Queen

CAMERON JAMES

SRL PUBLISHING

SRL Publishing Ltd
London
www.srlpublishing.co.uk

First published worldwide by SRL Publishing in 2023

ISBN: 978-191507317-4

1 3 5 7 9 10 8 6 4 2

A CIP catalogue record for this book is available from the
British Library

SRL Publishing is a Climate Positive publisher offsetting more
carbon emissions than it emits.

Content warnings: References to bullying, student/teacher
relationships, sex, suicide, HIV

To everybody who is searching for their word, I hope you find it.

One

I laughed, rubbing my hands over my face, pulling on my hair then holding my hands firm on my head. My chest rose and fell as I turned my head. Marley smiled back at me before lying back onto the pillow, closing his eyes as I looked around the room that we'd fallen into.

It was a spare bedroom, I think; it didn't appear to have any personality behind it. It definitely didn't belong to Lucah, whose house this was. The party was loud below and around us, the music almost making the floor vibrate, the sound of laughter distant from the room we were in.

Marley had found me. I hadn't been looking for sex, not tonight. I'd been stood with a vodka and Coke watching as my brother and his boyfriend thoroughly enjoyed the party and it had been amusing me, then Marley had appeared at my side, his own drink in hand, and we spoke.

We spoke about Christmas.

We spoke about his trip to see Hamilton over the

break.

We spoke about going back to school.

We spoke about what we thought the musical might be this coming summer.

Then, we kissed, and then we fell into this lacklustre bedroom.

There was a blower on the bedside table. Silver with multicoloured strips. I rose it to my lips. I blew into it, creating a light tooting sound, then laughed as Marley opened his eyes and looked at me. He grinned as I blew into it again, making a far better sound.

"Happy New Year," I whispered; Marley laughed, placing a kiss on my lips. I held the back of his head, keeping the kiss as tame as I could make it. When he moved away, lying back on the bed, I got up out of it and began to get dressed. I smiled at Marley as I pulled my cable-knit sweater over my head. I rubbed my hands over my arms before sitting on the bed to put on my shoes. I blew a kiss to him as I pulled my phone out of my jeans pocket and left the room.

Kennedy, my twin brother, the King, was leant against the wall in the hallway, on his own phone as he waited. I nudged his elbow. His arm rose and almost let go of his phone. He looked at me, then he smiled.

"What are you doing?" I whispered. He nodded to the door we were stood next to.

"Waiting for Stephen." He watched my face as I frowned. "This is the bathroom."

"Ah."

"Where have you been?"

"Bedroom," I murmured. "Marley."

He had a knowing look on his face, clearly understanding how we'd gotten into the bedroom, especially so early in the party. "Hey," he whispered, lifting my chin with his fist. I looked into his eyes. "Okay?"

"Okay," I agreed, then I laughed as if to prove I was, in fact, okay. "I'm just concerned Marley might start to believe we're exclusive. I can't have that."

"He adores you; you can see it in his eyes."

"He's good with his tongue, but no," I said simply. Kennedy smiled. "You, sweetheart, are the monogamous one." He laughed as the bathroom door opened. His boyfriend Stephen appeared through it, smiling.

They were our modern-day Romeo and Juliet case. Stephen, the goalkeeper of our school's football team, the lowest of the low in the school hierarchy, or at least they had been. Since his relationship with the King had been revealed to the entire school through a ridiculously romantic grand gesture planned by my brother, the football team had been gaining popularity in such a way that was unheard of.

My brother was the King. The, all things considered, highest of the high. He ruled the school and everybody in it, and he had done for the last three years. He was cool and collected. Well liked amongst our peers and completely fair in everything he did. He played the saxophone in our school orchestra; five-time national champions, thank you very much.

They were quite the handsome couple, which wasn't

3

lost on most of the school. The ideal couple to stick on the poster and proclaim that Happily Ever Afters exist.

I, however, was the Queen.

I ruled the theatre department, and most of the school behind Kennedy's back. I fitted more in to the villain role of the story. If Kennedy is the King, who gets his Prince Charming, I'm the Evil Queen who has a whole lot of sex, and shouts at mirrors for not telling me I'm beautiful. I wasn't due a happily ever after any time soon.

Especially not with Marley.

I sat in the garden as the countdown to midnight began, a bottle of beer between my first two fingers. A fire roared in a metal bin in front of me. Most of the boys from my theatre were sat around me, all with their own drinks.

Kennedy and Stephen sat on the garden chairs next to me, counting down from ten with the rest of the party.

Fireworks shot up into the sky, exploding in quick concession; boys kissed around me. Their boyfriends, their best friends or their fucks for the night.

I smiled softly as Kennedy wrapped his arms around Stephen. They shared a simple kiss and then a happy smile, leaning their foreheads against each other's, wishing the other a Happy New Year and many happy returns.

I drank more beer, almost choking on it as Kennedy stood from where he was sat, wrapping his arms around my body and kissing my cheek.

"Happy New Year, Queen," he said into my ear.

I wrapped my arms around his neck and placed a light peck on his lips. "Happy New Year, darling," I replied.

We sat before the principal and most of the teachers. We hardly saw the principal; I had to take a double take on the woman who wore a fierce pantsuit because I didn't recognise her as the head of our school. There were the heads of every subject, all sat looking as if they wished this meeting was already over.

There was the orchestra conductor, Otis.

The theatre director, Finn.

There was Kennedy, the King, and there was me, the Queen.

We'd been invited to the first staff meeting of the year, because it was getting dangerously close to us leaving the school and decisions had to be made. It turned out the teaching staff cared more about the student monarchy than any of us ever realised. It turned out, whoever the most popular student was had a huge impact on how the school was viewed.

Currently, the school had quite a solid reputation, with the twin sons of the one-day prime minister, both of them openly gay, one of them a prize-winning saxophonist, the other a strong support of trans rights and the lead of the theatre.

We represented current politics – although somewhat unwillingly – LGBTQ representation, and support for the arts. We kept the funding rolling in, all things considered.

Now, we needed a new King, who would rule as fairly as Kennedy and as freely as me.

"Are any of the young men in the band... eligible?" the principal asked. Otis rifled through his pages.

Kennedy seemed thoughtful. "Who's the next oldest?" he asked.

Otis laughed. "Oh no, son, we're not leaving the school to Georgie," he said.

"I retract that so *hard*; Georgie is the next oldest, my god," Kennedy said, laughing.

"Exactly," Otis mused. Finn smirked at me and I bit my lip so I wouldn't laugh out loud.

"What about Malakai?" I said. Kennedy and Otis seemed surprised. "Isn't he a businessman's son?"

"I think so," Otis said, "and a stunning violinist."

The table seemed to agree. Kennedy squeezed my knee in approval.

"How old is he, Otis?" Finn asked.

Otis raised his eyes to the sky, as if asking God for the answer. "Fifteen," he said warily.

"Malakai Anderson?" the subject lead of English said. "He's fifteen. He's in my fourth year English."

"Good choice, Queen," Finn said. I winked at him.

"Yes, good suggestion Cassidy." The principal smiled, a warm smile, so I returned it.

I closed my locker, then I jumped, laughing softly to try my damned best to disguise the fact that my soul had just left my body in fright.

"Archie," I purred.

Archie grinned back at me, his braces twinkling in the artificial light of the corridors. He hugged his books to his chest, his eyes wide as they always were. "Did you have a good Christmas my Queen?" he asked, a joking tone to his voice that had only developed this year – the joking tone that is, *not* his voice. That was yet to break.

"Oh yes, yourself peasant?"

He laughed, the sound happy. "I thought I had been promoted to your servant," he said.

"True," I said lightly, then kissed his cheek. They instantly turned bright red, his shoulders raising to almost his ears. God he was adorable.

He'd found me on his second day of his first year. I'd just been crowned Queen, and the auditions for the theatre were coming up. The first few weeks of school buzz was everywhere, and I'd had many younger years linger around me, trying to get a place in the ensemble.

Archie appeared beside my locker a little bit lost, and a whole lot scared, clutching onto a book of the musical CATS, and not much else. He hadn't been purposely looking for me; no, he'd been looking for the theatre, because he wanted to audition and he didn't want to be late.

I told him he was lucky, as that was where I was going.

He asked if he could come with me.

He got into the ensemble, blowing Finn and me away despite his nerves and tremors, and then he kind of stuck. He had friends of his own, I *knew* that; he hung around with the other boys in his year who had got into the theatre, but he always appeared beside me at least once a day, to give me updates, to let me know what everyone is whispering about. He was like my own Zazu delivering me the morning report.

He was thirteen now, third year, and I wish him King one day, but a theatre boy had never been King and I didn't know if that'd ever change. Maybe he'd make a nice Queen after all.

"Is Theo enjoying New York?"

"I would think so," I said. "He'll be back by next week. Is that all anyone's talking about?"

"No, the obvious is still buzzing."

"Kennedy and Stephen?"

"Yeah. Mostly positive. Whispers of Devon."

"Why?" I asked as I closed my locker.

"Falling from grace, should I say? It's becoming public knowledge what he did to Kennedy. There were still some blurred lines, but now I think most know."

"Interesting," I said cheerfully. "Thank you baby, you're invaluable to me."

He buried his nose in his books, but smiled none the less. I went to walk away, but he reached for my arm. "I wanted to tell you something else," he said, then quickly took his hand off my arm. I nodded to him, telling him to go ahead. "I'm..." He paused then closed his eyes. "Fuck's sake."

I laughed, covering my mouth with my hand. "Archie sweetheart, what is it?"

He sighed, keeping his eyes closed. "I'm gay," he said quickly.

It took all my effort not to point out he was stating the obvious. Instead, I hugged him. He squeaked in excitement. "I'm so proud of you. Is there a boy, is that why?"

"Yes," he said shyly. "Updates will come as they happen."

"Who is it?" I asked. He sighed as he flushed. "I could put in a good word."

"No, no Cassidy," he said, laughing. "No, I love you, Queen, but please don't."

I crossed my heart. He smiled.

"Oscar," he said, then sighed.

"In the theatre?"

"He's the year below me," he whispered. "I don't know if... it can happen."

"It can," I said, "and if it's meant to, it will."

"Really?"

"Like Kennedy and Stephen..." I said. "Like me and..."

"Why aren't you boys in the theatre? Isn't that where you're supposed to be?" Finn asked.

"Isn't that where *you're* supposed to be?" I replied. Finn quirked his eyebrow at me, waving his arm in the direction of the theatre, so we went.

"You and who?" Archie asked as we walked behind Finn.

I looked at him, then at Finn. "Me and the role of Anne Boleyn, of course," I said.

Archie laughed cheerfully. "Of course."

He practically skipped through the door Finn was

holding open to the theatre. I stepped through after him, smiling at Finn as he passed me half the sheets in his hands.

Kennedy and Cody were talking, throwing a ball back and forth between their beds as their conversation grew excited and louder, interspersed with manic laughter. I had sat and listened for some of the conversation but soon grew bored, lifting my headphones over my ears and blasting the *Waitress* soundtrack around my head.

I tuned in occasionally, especially when Kennedy mentioned Stephen, intrigued but zoning out pretty quickly. I missed Theo.

It had been the four of us in this room since our first day of first year. Kennedy and me, Cody the celloist in the orchestra and Theo, a theatre boy like me. Theo was my *very* best friend who knew the deepest, darkest secrets about me, and currently he was galivanting around New York to celebrate his eighteenth birthday.

I was envious and I wasn't hiding it, and I felt like pouting because Kennedy had his best friend Cody and I didn't have anyone to play with, so instead I blasted the delicious tones of Jessie Mueller and actually attempted to complete my homework, because I literally had *nothing* better to do.

I jumped when I was touched, looking up then throwing my headphones off and leaping on Theo as he laughed and hugged me back.

"When did you get home?"

"Just." He shook his head. "Yesterday. I've literally

been sleeping all day. Dad woke me up, told me I better get to school." He laughed as I hugged him again.

"Tell me all about it. I need to know everything. What was Broadway like? Times Square? The Empire State?"

"It was…" He sighed contently. "Incredible."

Two

Theo continued to talk. I'm sure if I was listening, I'd have been fully intrigued, even actively engaged in the conversation, but my attention was focused on Finn as he leant against the exit door to the theatre. He had a folder in his arms, a few papers on top that he was rifling through. He looked up; he must have felt my eyes on him, as he found me quickly.

I smiled.

He laughed as he bit his lip, then came towards Theo and me. I didn't break our eye contact as I pulled a cigarette out of the box in my pocket, tapping it against the cardboard before putting it in my mouth.

"Smoking on campus," he said, looking over my shoulder to Theo, who laughed but didn't hide his mostly smoked cigarette. "That's not allowed." He tutted, looking back towards me.

"Oops," I whispered as I lifted the box to him. His eyes dropped down to the box instantly. "I guess you don't want one then," I added. Theo hit my shoulder so I smiled; it was sweet, I guess.

Finn put his finger on his lips, then used the finger to pull a cigarette out of the box.

"Got a light?" he asked as he rose the cigarette to his lips. I smiled at him, putting my own back into my mouth and showing him my zippo lighter, gold with *Queen* engraved into its body, a crown above the words. I flipped open the top, the flame growing and flickering. We leant in at the same time, the flame catching the end of both our cigarettes. I rose my eyes to him, winking at him as we moved our heads away, both taking the cigarettes out of our mouths and blowing away the smoke.

"I feel a bit like a leftover part," Theo mused.

I turned to him, gasping as I did. "Never, my darling Theodore," I said.

"Darling, we could cut the tension with a knife," he said. I rose my eyebrow at him as Finn laughed.

"I don't know what you're talking about, Theo," Finn said. "Simply sharing a cigarette with students. Totally above board," he joked. Theo laughed, and I smiled, looking down at my shoes. "Speaking of actually, Cassidy I want to pick your brain."

"Oh yeah?" I asked, lifting my head. "And how would you like to do that darling?"

"Come visit me in my office, after lessons, please."

"Your wish is my command." I practically purred at him. He laughed, his cheeks flushing, but to Theo it could've been the cold. I mean, of course it was the cold. Finn nodded to us both, smoking the end of his cigarette before putting it out on the bin we were stood next to. He winked at me as he walked away. I grinned at him, bringing my cigarette back to my lips.

I knocked in a sort of rat-a-tat way on Finn's office door. He called out to me, granting me entry, so I opened the door, closing it slowly behind me. I pushed it shut with both of my hands until it clicked, then I flipped over the lock.

Finn laughed behind me, so I turned as he collected highlighted sheets that were scattered around his desk. "I'm thinking a lot about the summer musical."

"Of course, that makes perfect sense," I said as I walked towards his desk. "You wanted to pick my brain." I pushed back his stationary pot then sat on his desk. I watched as his eyes roamed over me, and I smiled at him, crossing my right leg over my left and leaning my elbow on my knee, my chin on my elbow. "What are the options?" I asked.

"*Carrie.*"

"No," I said.

He laughed as he tapped the papers against the desk, straightening them before placing them down. "*Be More Chill.*"

"Oh, interesting," I said. He looked up at me and our eyes met. "Really."

"*How to Succeed in Business.*"

"Very male," I said almost frowning at him.

He laughed as he walked around his desk until he was stood in front of me. "Very good observation," he said, a slight lint in his voice. He rested his hand on my knee.

I rose my head, putting my hands on the desk. "Do I get to choose the cast?" I asked.

"Hmm, no." His hand slid down my thigh. I uncrossed my legs.

"Why don't I get to choose the cast?"

"You get to choose what you sing?" he said as his other hand touched my other thigh, his hands roaming up my legs at a similar speed. "The entire musical, or 'Michael in the Bathroom'," he said.

I laughed, leaning my head back as I did. "Oh that's… tough, sweetheart," I whispered.

He wrapped his hands around my back and pulled me forward. "I guess you'll have to think about it." He pulled me close enough that he could stand against me, and I could feel him, his breath near my ear, his chest rising and falling against mine, his hardness. I ran my fingers delicately over his arms, up towards his shoulders, until I could stroke my finger through the buzzed hair near the top of his neck. "A very hard decision, I would imagine."

I laughed softly, not wanting to disturb the silence of the room. We were playing, we both knew it. We were playing a very gay and dangerous game of chicken. Who'd crack first and kiss the other. Given his hardness and my resilience, I figured it'd be him.

I mean, he'd lost the last three times.

"Your dirty talk is atrocious," I whispered straight into his ear.

"Like you can do any better."

He sounded like he was sulking, and I couldn't have

that, so I ran my finger from his neck down his chin, lifting it so he was looking straight at me.

"Don't pout," I said, then stroked my thumb over his lips. He opened his mouth very slightly, his tongue darting out. I grinned at him, holding his chin between my finger and thumb, pulled his head towards me, and kissed him.

Finn: 5. Cassidy: 3.

My hand slid up, my fingers getting lost in his hair as his hands slid under my blazer until he was touching my back, his fingers searching around my shirt until he could touch skin.

"I don't need to dirty talk," I whispered as I broke the kiss to breathe. He bit his lip. "I simply just show you," I said as if I was providing a fucking service. He laughed, his hands under the shoulders of my blazer. He lifted them, my blazer sliding down my arms, so I threw it away from us. I laughed giddily as he tugged on my shirt, untucking it from my pants. He smirked at me; it was deliciously evil as he lifted my shirt.

I gasped when he tweaked my nipple piercing, twisting it in his fingers, sending a sharp zap of *pleasurepain* through my body. My back arched into him, and it satisfied him far too damn much, but we groaned out together. His was cut off when his mouth was on my nipple, his tongue wrapped around my piercing. The feeling of the *pleasurepain* fluttered deep in my stomach, and I grasped a fistful of his hair. I closed my eyes and opened my mouth in an inaudible gasp. Until:

"Fuck." He laughed against my chest and I pulled his

head away, kissing him messily. "Condom." His eyes danced as if he wanted to try and tell me to be patient, but it was almost as if he wouldn't dare, and I liked that because it meant I'd trained him well.

He took my hand in his, stroking over my palm before slipping my hand into his pocket. I smiled as I pulled out the square foiled packet. "Prepared, I like it."

"I know," he said, his voice almost a growl, making me shiver. "I didn't want to be told off again." I laughed very openly at him.

"You should've been more prepared." I tutted, shaking my head at him as I held the condom up to him. I rose my eyebrow; he sucked on his bottom lip as he reached for the belt on his slacks. It came apart with a clank of metal on metal. "I mean, how hard is it to pick up a condom," I teased as I ran my finger over the foil, my thumb over the ring of the condom. He laughed, and it almost sounded breathless. I grinned a sweet-as-sugar grin at him as he unzipped his trousers, pushing them and his boxers down in one fluid movement.

Then, I moaned.

"Such a pretty dick," I said as if it physically hurt me. "I just want it inside me." I tore open the condom packet. He watched as I stroked down his dick, then rolled the condom down, ensuring I added pressure before squeezing when I got to the base of his dick.

He made the slightest of choked noises in the back of his throat. I lifted his chin.

"How do you want me?" I asked.

He laughed. "I get a choice?"

"Of course you do, baby doll. You can have me this way." I opened my legs just that bit further. "Or, I could turn around and we can do it up against your desk. I know how you like that." I kissed his cheek, almost innocently. He sighed, pulling me off the desk and turning me around.

I smiled as I knew he couldn't see my face, then aided him by undoing my trousers. Sighing with relief when my dick was finally free, I gave it a dry tug, feeling it resonate low and suppressing the groan as best I could. He laughed somewhere behind me, the sound almost loving. I turned my head to look at him as he squirted lube onto his hand, his fingers slick.

He rested his unlubricated hand on the small of my back, his thumb stroking my back as one of his fingers entered me.

"Good?" he whispered.

I nodded, laughing with a gasp when a second finger entered me. "Good." I couldn't see his smirk, but I could sure as hell feel it.

"Only the best for the Queen," he teased. I laughed, closing my eyes, but not for long. He reangled his fingers and I wanted to come right there and then. "Got you," he whispered.

I growled at him. "Fuck me."

"Oh, I will." He leant closer to me, his hardness bumping against me, then he kissed my cheek. "All in good time."

I wanted to whine, but I remembered I was the Queen, and the Queen didn't wait to be fucked. She did the fucking, so I moved back into him, his fingers going just that bit deeper, and I moaned, long and loud. He laughed, and it sounded pained. His fingers were gone.

I whimpered, low in my throat at the loss of his finger, then gasped as I was filled up to the brim with his dick. His hand clasped around my shirt, scrunching it into his fist and tugging it to anchor himself.

"Better?" he growled.

"Much better."

I sat on his desk chair in my shirt and boxers, my right leg over the arm of the chair, my left towards my body. He was sat on his desk, his undershirt and his trousers on, and a smile on his face that I couldn't look at for too long because it was beautiful and I wanted to coo at him.

"I think Theo would kill 'Michael in the Bathroom'," I said as I played with the bottom of my tie.

"Which gives you the lead," he said.

"Oh, look at that." He laughed softly and I looked back at his face. "Hey, at least I deserve it."

"True," he muttered. "Very true. And we have to get our fill of Cassidy before you go."

"Exactly," I said. "Just think about the gaping hole in the school when I'm gone."

"Gaping hole is right."

"That was rude," I said sarcastically, and he laughed cheerfully. "True, but rude."

"Well, what can I say." He shrugged. "I'm nothing if I'm not honest."

"Totally," I agreed. "And how honest it is to be

fucking a student." He kicked the chair so it rocked, and I wish I hadn't screamed but I did and he began to laugh.

"You can hardly be counted as a student," he muttered.

I lifted my tie to him. "I'm merely eighteen," I teased, and he smirked. "Imagine if my father knew… Oh let's tell my father."

"Cassidy."

"Anything to piss off Father," I muttered, then I sighed as I turned towards my phone. It vibrated vigorously but ignored it.

"You're not a Jeremy, my dear. You, however, would be an incredible Squib."

"Yeah?"

He nodded. "Definitely. You're not soft enough to be Jeremy, but you are hot enough to be the Squib."

I laughed until my phone started vibrating again, so I stood from the chair and got it out of my pants, I saw *The King* and the crown emoji flashing on my screen.

I walked towards Finn and kissed him, and he made a surprised noise but kissed me back. I pulled away, smiled pleasantly at him then covered his mouth with my hand. He frowned, then rolled his eyes as I called Kennedy back.

"Yes, my brother?"

Kennedy laughed into my ear. "Where are you?"

"Busy," I said, my eyes slowly tracking over Finn as he blew against my hand.

"Before, during or after?" he asked.

I smirked. "All done and dusted, my love."

"Are you coming to dinner?"

"Probably. I am hungry." Finn sighed against my hand. "I will finish up here, take the scenic route and see you in the dining room." Finn licked my hand.

"Okay," Kennedy said, and I could feel the smile in his voice so I smiled back.

"Bye, baby."

"Bye, sweetheart," he replied, then hung up. I took my hand away from Finn's mouth, wiping it down his face. "You think licking my hand is going to make me scream?" I said, and he shook his head as I walked towards my trousers, stepping into them.

"No, but licking your asshole will."

I don't know how I didn't fall over. "Next time," I said as I zipped up my trousers. "You promise?" I walked towards him, tucking my shirt in.

"Promise," he purred at me.

I picked up my blazer and put it back on before sitting on his desk chair to put my shoes on. "Goodbye, my love," I said, kissing him lightly, with just lips. I went to walk away but he grabbed onto my arm, pulling me back.

"Ah-ah, it's going to be at least a week until I get you like this again. Kiss me properly."

"Sir," I teased; he narrowed his eyes so I pulled my tongue. He caught it, kissing me deeply, his hands tight on my hips. I tried to focus; I didn't want all the blood in my body rush to my groin. I was very much up for a round two; however, it wouldn't have been wise. "Calm down there, sir," I whispered close to his ear. "I have the stamina for a round two, but I wouldn't want to wear you out."

"You little shit," he growled at me his hands grabbing my ass.

"Don't worry darling, you're not eighteen anymore."

"Watch your mouth, Queen," he said, and I smiled as I stepped around the desk back towards the door.

"Goodbye baby," I whispered, blowing a kiss to him. He caught it as he stood from his desk, sitting back on the chair as I left. I grinned, closing the door behind me and leant back on it. I took a deep breath, smiled, then reached into my pocket for my carton of cigarettes.

Three

I knew the boy in front of me. I was sure of it. I knew the blonde hair and the lightly sun-kissed skin. I knew the brown eyes that were scanning the menu even though they'd already placed their order. I knew everything about this boy; I just couldn't quite place him.

He walked away from the cashier, waiting for his coffee at the other end of the counter, and I watched, until the unnecessarily pretty barista asked for my order.

Hazelnut latte, grande.

I followed the boy down the counter until I was stood next to him. Oh, I knew exactly who he was.

"Gotten over your recent disaster of a concert?" I said as I played with a wooden stirrer. The boy, the boy who was called Cameron, a student of Goldstein Institute of Music and Theatre for boys, turned to look at me, a frown on his devastatingly pretty face. It let up almost instantly as he saw me, because he definitely knew who I was.

"Excuse me?" he said.

"You can hardly talk with how sloppy your recent attempt was."

"Sloppy?" I repeated, then I laughed. "Oh, baby doll, you are deluded if you think we were sloppy." His eyes roamed me, and I let him because it'd taken me a solid half an hour to put together my outfit. "Poor really for a specialist school, don't you think?" I teased.

"You were okay, for a community group," he said, and I almost choked.

"Bitch, please," I said, my voice almost shrill. He smirked, then turned to walk past me.

"Don't you have a saxophone you need to… rehearse," he said, and I stopped him.

"Wait, what?"

He rolled his eyes. "I know what a saxophone is, you're never going…"

"That's not me," I said, and he turned to fully face me. "That's my twin, Kennedy." He frowned and I said, "You're Cameron, aren't you?" As if to confirm, he turned his cup towards me. *Casper* was written in sharpie, a heart in place of the 'a'.

"Twin," he said.

"What?"

"Grande hazelnut latte," the barista called. I turned towards it, retrieving my coffee, and I watched Casper read it.

"Cassidy?" he said. I nodded; my 'a' was a heart too. "I didn't even know Kennedy had a twin."

"I didn't know Cameron did," I said, and he laughed,

covering his mouth with his hand.

"So, we've just stood here and shit-talked the wrong person."

"Yeah," I said. "That's embarrassing." "Wait, you're in Goldstein's orchestra?"

"Trumpet," he said, then took a sip out of his coffee. "I presume you're a Ravenwood Theatre Boy."

"*The* Ravenwood theatre boy," I replied, and he laughed. "Do you want to get a drink?" I asked.

He raised his eyebrows and lifted his cup towards me. "One step ahead of you."

"Oh, yeah, course." I inwardly shunned myself because we were already in a damn coffee shop.

"I'll happily drink it with you though," he said, then he looked at the floor. "Now that I know you're not your saxophone-playing brother."

I smiled as I played with the lid of my coffee cup. "And you're not your surprisingly talented brother."

"Cam would be over the moon to hear that," he said. I gasped, and he imitated me in a mocking way. I decided I liked Casper. "I know, right, you just complimented a Golden Boy."

"Strip me of my kingdom," I said, and he laughed, looking away from me, taking a sip out of his cup then reaching into his pocket.

"I've—"

"Got to go," I said, finishing his sentence for him. He looked a bit saddened by this, so I put my hand out to him. He didn't question me as he placed his phone into the palm of my hand. I typed my number in. "I'll get you that coffee at some point," I said, and he smiled as he took his phone back.

"It's a date." He winked at me before leaving the coffee shop. I smiled after him then reached for my own phone, reading the first few words of a text from Theo.

I walked to meet him, smiling as I approached him. He pushed himself from where he was leaning on a wall, smoking a cigarette. My phone vibrated in my pocket as I reached him.

I took it out, then I laughed.

Unknown Number: Not Cameron.

I grinned as Theo stubbed out the end of his cigarette.

"Flirting?"

"For once, no," I said, pocketing my phone again. "Shopping." He nodded in agreement, linking his arm around mine, and we started down Oxford Street.

I laughed when my phone buzzed, simply a text from Father telling me he wished to speak to me. He'd send a town car and he expected me to be in it.

I told him I couldn't *possibly* travel all the way from London to Brighton; my schooling was far too important.

He called bullshit but informed me we'd be meeting in central London. I got in the town car.

He met me at a restaurant. A high-profile place that didn't put the price next to the menu items.

He was sat, a bottle of wine at the table, the menu resting on his plate. He barely acknowledged me as I approached him, and looked unimpressed when I sat down without announcing myself.

His eyes met mine for the briefest of seconds before I was handed a menu.

Our father was a successful man. An outstanding citizen who was destined to be prime minister one day. He was presentable, well put together, wore expensive suits and had an expensive haircut. He looked the part. He truly did. He'd been educated in Ravenwood, much like Kennedy and me, much like our older brother Harrison. He'd graduated with references and honours, far too many to name. He knew what to say in any situation. I'd marvelled at it as a child, watching our father stand before huge crowds and speak with ease. As I'd got older, I began to appreciate how much of an act it was. That he was hiding behind something, like me being stood on the stage; like me being the Queen.

Our father resembled Harrison, I think: tall, broad and dark haired. Kennedy and I looked like our mum: tall, but slight with ginger hair and green eyes.

I ordered the lamb rack; he ordered the marinated tuna.

"Cassidy," he said, and I looked up at him expectantly as wine was poured into my glass. I thanked the wait staff and took a sip.

"Yes, Father?" I asked.

He rolled his eyes. "We've had this conversation more times than I can count, son," he said in a

27

diplomatic voice. I frowned at him, feigning ignorance at what was about to come. "You are given an allowance. Quite a substantial allowance. You are not required to pay for boarding, or for meals. You're not required to pay any living costs. So I need to ask, what are you spending your allowance on?"

"Why?" I asked.

"I received a bill yesterday," he said. "Made to my checking account, from Selfridges, from Harrods. For quite substantial amounts. So, pray tell, what do you spend your allowance on, Cassidy?"

I smirked behind the wine glass, holding it to my mouth. "Nothing," I said lightly.

"Kennedy doesn't use my checking account."

"Ah, yes, because Kennedy is the golden twin, of course," I said. He sighed, sitting upright, so I copied as our plates were placed in front of us.

"If Kennedy can survive off his allowance, then you—"

"Oh, I can survive. My allowance is lovely and cushy, but I have to look good, don't you think? You can't have me attending public events in the same suit as last time."

He stared me out as I cut into the lamb. "A school party is hardly a public event."

"People will see me; do you know there's an entire blog about my outfits? I have a reputation to uphold."

"You have a cheek," he said, and I looked away. "I will cut you off."

"You won't, not yet, anyway."

"Cassidy," he growled, then cleared his throat and

regained his posture.

"It's not as if you don't have the money."

"That isn't the point," he stated. "I donate a lot to you, to Kennedy. A lot to Ravenwood. I pay the thousands of pounds for his saxophones, for your scenery and your light and sound equipment. I pay a lot in; I should not have my son stealing from me."

I rose an eyebrow at him, and he looked thoroughly unimpressed that I wasn't fighting back. If you wanted a fight, you came to me; everyone knew that what I lacked in physical strength I had in a sharp tongue, but I learnt quite early on not to fight with Father, not until I could survive from my own wealth, at least.

"You can borrow the clothes, if you want to get your money's worth?" I said, then drank from the wine.

"You think you're funny?"

"No, not at all. In fact, quite the opposite."

"You're on your last warning, Cassidy. You hear me? If I get one more bill from you, you will be cut off. Your card, your allowance, *everything* will be cut off and I will have no remorse doing so."

"Mum wouldn't let you."

"It's my money, your mother has no say in the matter. She'll understand I'm trying to teach my son a lesson in respect."

"Respect?" I repeated, laughing. "I have a whole lot of respect."

"One more bill. You're cut off," he said simply. "I'm not joking, Cassidy."

Four

Little paper hearts littered my locker. Some were handmade, some shop bought; they all had declarations of love on them. I looked at the one in the middle, smiling at Archie's familiar scrawl. It simply read;

You know the love I have for my Queen. A x

Some were from younger years, some from boys in my year. Some were anonymous and I couldn't decode the handwriting of them.

"Ah, your adoring fans," Theo sang at me as he walked around me to his own locker. To his credit, his also had some hearts on, and they were mostly sweet. He detached one, his cheeks flushing warmly as he read it. I watched him until he turned back to me. He opened his mouth to say something to me, but ultimately decided against it, swallowing down the words, so I didn't ask.

Not yet, at least.

"Are you going to the Valentine's Party?" I asked.

Theo nodded slowly. "Myles hosting?"

"No," I said, surprised. Theo laughed. "Lucah."

"Since when did Lucah host parties?" he asked, pulling his books out of his locker and leaning against it to shut it.

I shook my head. "I don't know, but have you seen his house? It's incredible."

"Good," he said.

I smiled. "Who are you going with?"

"No one," he said without looking up at me.

"Okay...Who do you want to go with?" I asked, and he laughed.

"Nope," he said simply then kissed my cheek, walking around me towards his Maths lesson. I watched him go, sighing as he did. He turned out of my sight as Finn came into it, walking down the corridor towards me. I smiled then schooled my face as he reached me.

"Cassidy," he said.

"Finn." He smiled as he stopped, turning to look at me; his eyes, however, drifted to my locker, his eyebrow raising in amusement as he looked over the hearts.

"Popular."

"Come on, Finn, we already know this." He laughed, shaking his head. "In fact, I'm one of the most popular in school," I added, taking a step towards him. He smirked at me, clearing his throat.

"Auditions are coming up, popular kid," he said, passing me the poster he had. I smiled at it. "Be there."

I nodded, biting my lip lightly as I did.

I swear he took another step towards me. If we took *another* step, we'd be chest to chest. Instead, I took a step back as Devon, the self-proclaimed Princess of the school, stopped near his locker.

I glared towards him, for no real reason except I'd prefer to step in shit than see his face. Finn turned, seeing Devon, then nodded to me before continuing on. I watched him go, then followed, walking past Devon, ignoring him as his gaze followed me.

I took a deep breath as I straightened my bow tie. It was navy blue, with red and white hearts all over it. My shirt was a powder pink, my slacks a heather grey and turned up at the ankle, my braces white, my Chuck Taylors white. I was going to make everyone regret making me walk into this party alone.

I fixed my hair.

Brushed my teeth.

Sprayed myself with cologne then opened the door to the bathroom.

"Well, are we ready?" I asked. Theo turned to look at me, and we smiled at each other. He was wearing white dungarees, a rip in his right knee, a pink t-shirt underneath and white Vans. He looked amazing, and I told him as much.

Kennedy and Cody, however...

"You're going like that?" I asked, and my brother had the audacity to roll his eyes.

Cody looked amused. "Yes," he replied as he walked

towards me, wrapping his arms around me and swaying us side to side. He was wearing a long hoodie that reached his thighs. It was a beautiful baby blue, but I refused to tell him the colour was beautiful; he'd matched it with grey skinny jeans and a pair of trainers, and sure, he looked good, but he wasn't dressed for a Valentine's Party.

Kennedy wasn't much better in a blue jumper with white stripes from the chest to the hem, jeans, and his Doc Martens. It was almost as if neither of them had put any effort in.

"It's not going to get much better, is it?" I asked Cody, and he shook his head, so I sighed. He kissed my cheek then laughed, spinning me out of his grip and towards Theo, whose arms I linked with. We walked out of our room together.

Lucah lived in a big, detached house. It was flat and square, with twelve rectangular windows looking out onto the street, and it was so wide, it seemed to go on and on for miles.

It was full. There were boys sat on the stairs, stood in doorways, picking from the catering station, filling up their pink cups with alcohol. Some were dancing in the front room, little coloured lights chasing themselves around the room from the floor to the ceiling as the music made the floor vibrate.

The back room was far more relaxed with people sat drinking on the couches, talking and laughing. Lucah was amongst them, looking pleased with how his party was progressing around him. I waved to him, a twinkly thing that made him laugh and wave back, lifting his cup as if telling me to get a drink, so I nodded, turning to Kennedy.

"Drink?" I asked. He nodded, slipping his phone back into his pocket and following me into the kitchen.

"Are you drinking?"

"Definitely," I said in a sigh. I looked through the spirits until I settled on the vodka. He filled his with Jack Daniels. "If I'm not hungover tomorrow I've done tonight wrong," I said. A laugh passed across Kennedy's face then he jumped and turned, wrapping his arms around Stephen and laughing as they spun together. Then they kissed. I sighed and drank some of the vodka straight.

Stephen turned to look at me when they broke the kiss, smiling at me, so I grinned back.

"So weird being able to walk through a popular guy's party and not be stopped," he said, then frowned at Kennedy. "I feel like Mia Thermopolis."

"Who?" Kennedy asked, and I gasped.

"Anne Hathaway," I said. "*The Princess Diaries*."

"You saw me when I was invisible," Stephen said, then he tutted. "Ew, I chose the wrong twin."

"That has always been evident to me," I said then poured the Coke into my cup. "Have fun, baby doll," I added, winking at Stephen as Kennedy complained at him.

I went into the back room. Three other boys stood from their seats when I walked in. I smiled at them all, stroking my fingers across the shoulders of the boy whose seat I took. He smiled like he'd won a prize when I took his seat, then he sat on the floor.

"What were we talking about in here?" I asked, taking another sip from my cup.

"I'm trying to persuade this lot to play truth or dare," Lucah stated with exasperation.

"Oh," I said, "consider my interest piqued, but maybe something a bit more exciting, no?"

"Like, your Majesty?" Lucah asked, and we smiled at each other.

"Spin the bottle," we said at the same time.

We sat in a large circle, surrounding an empty bottle of vodka that Lucah had spun around a few times to make sure it had a good spin on it.

"Rules as follows," Lucah said, and I nodded.

"Truth or kiss. Pick kiss, you spin. First kiss is a peck, second if it lands on the same person again is a kiss lasting a minute, third, tongues," I said, lowering all three of my fingers as the circle nodded in agreement. "If you pick truth, the person who spun it so it landed on you asks your truth. Got it?"

"Got it," Lucah said, then he spun the bottle. It landed on Marley.

"Truth or Kiss?" I asked. Marley's eyes examined me, roaming my entire body, then he looked back at Lucah.

"Truth," he said. Lucah smirked because best friends were the *worst*.

"Out of everybody here," Lucah said. Marley nodded

35

slowly, his tongue wetting his lips as he did. "Who do you want to sleep with?" he asked. Marley laughed, although it sounded more like a cough. He looked around the entire circle as if this was an episode of *Take Me Out* and he had to turn off our lights.

His eyes jumped to the door once the circle was complete. I turned to look, smiling as Theo came and sat beside me.

"Rowan," Marley said, his eyes never leaving Theo. Lucah laughed as Rowan blew a kiss to him.

"Bitch," Lucah stated, "you're not touching my boyfriend."

Marley winked back at him.

"Who did you want me to say?" he asked as he knelt up and spun the bottle again.

"Cassidy," Lucah muttered, and I laughed.

"Honey, he doesn't need to pine after me, he's already been there," I purred, and Lucah looked impressed.

"Twice," Marley intoned as the bottle landed on Myles.

It landed on me the fifth spin. I looked at the end of the bottle before smirking with a hint of evil.

"Kiss," I said. The circle vibrated as I knelt up, letting my hand slide over the bottle before spinning it.

It landed on Peyton. I grinned at him, and he grinned straight back. Peyton was the pianist in the band, a beautiful pianist at that. He always tended to drift more towards my little group of theatre babies rather than

Kennedy's band boys, but he was pretty and he fitted right in.

He came to me – I didn't even need to tell him. He got straight out of his seat, stepped over the bottle, lifted my chin and placed a soft kiss on my lips.

It landed on Theo when I spun it again.

"Truth or Kiss?" I asked him, and he looked back at me as he bit his lip, then he sighed.

"Truth."

"Oh," I said, my voice high as a look of pure fear fell over his face. I decided not to be too cruel. I could've asked him who the heart that made him blush was from. I could've asked him who he liked, and he'd have lied straight to my face because he'd be obliged to give me an answer but not want to jeopardise whatever was going on. I appreciated that; in fact I respected that, so I asked:

"Have you ever sent a nude over Snapchat?"

Because I knew the answer.

"Yes," he said straight to me. Rowan coughed.

"Couldn't hear that sunshine? Nude, snapchat?"

"Yes," Theo repeated louder. He smiled at me even though it appeared brief, then he turned to the circle. "It was hot, too," he added.

"Kind of was," I said.

Theo laughed as he reached for the bottle. He rested his hand on it. "Any follow up questions?"

"Yeah…" Lucah said. Theo looked at him. "Who did you send it to?"

"Cassidy," Theo said playfully as he spun the bottle, sitting back on his heels, "and… Kennedy."

I laughed in a bark because I hadn't known it'd gone to Kennedy too. He grinned at me; it was full of mischief as the bottle landed on Peyton.

"Kiss," he said to Theo, tilting his head before spinning the bottle himself. It landed on me. The circle all hollered as Peyton shrugged at me, and I did it back.

I walked Peyton back until his back was straight against the wall. He watched me, his eyes darting over my entire body then over my shoulders as if to keep surveillance for us. I stroked my finger over his lips.

"No one's coming," I whispered, then I laughed, looking away from him. "Not yet, anyway."

"That..." he said, and I looked back at him. "That was seedy for the Queen."

"How dare you," I gasped in fake outrage, and he grinned as I kissed him. He moaned into my mouth, his hands clasping around my braces and holding them in his fists, not letting up as we made out. I moved away from him, smiling as he attempted to search out another kiss.

His eyes opened when it didn't come. I smiled at him as I slid my hands down his stomach until I could pull open his jeans. I sighed contentedly as his jeans came open through a simple tug of five buttons. He watched with interest, his expression verging on confused until I knelt before him and he *got* it. His head hit the wall behind him as I licked his dick through his boxers.

He moaned at me, his fingers weaving through my hair, grabbing on tightly. He pushing me towards his dick and I laughed.

"All in good time, baby. All in good time," I said, and he looked down at me through half-lidded eyes. I bit my tongue, grinning at him as I did.

I passed Kennedy and Stephen falling into a room as I left towards the kitchen. I smirked at Kennedy as he glanced at me over Stephen's shoulder, his face red as our eyes met, so I winked at him, laughed and continued on. I passed Cody as he flirted up a storm with Myles. They both looked amused and Cody laughed as he looked up at me and took a sip from his drink.

I passed Theo, squeezing his elbow as I did so he turned to look at me. I picked up a new pink cup, filling it almost halfway with vodka before adding a splash of Coke.

Someone was shaking my shoulder, their hand soft and gentle but the shake evident as they tried to wake me up.

All I could think was *leave me alone to die* because *my god* did I feel like I was dying. My head was pulsing so hard it made my nose hurt. My throat was raw and scratchy, my eyes heavy. I groaned back at whoever it was, and they laughed, their fingers stroking through my hair.

"Cassidy, baby," Theo said softly. I buried myself further into my pillow. "It's the afternoon," he whispered, and I laughed as I rubbed my eyes.

"Cassidy is hungover; please leave a message and I'll get back to you when I can formulate sentences."

"That was a pretty formulated sentence," Kennedy said. I opened one eye. He was sat on his bed, dressed.

"Didn't Stephen come back with you?"

"Yes. He left this *morning*, for football practice."

"I got you a Starbucks," Theo said.

"You're my favourite," I replied, and he reached for my bedside table, showing me the white cup with *Theo* written over the logo. He held it just far enough away from me that I'd have to sit up to get it.

I did but I also bitched about it.

"Do you even remember last night?"

"Yes," I said, sounding piss-proud of myself. Theo laughed. "We went to Lucah's party. I drank. We played spin the bottle. You admitted to sending a nude to Kennedy once..." I said. Theo laughed as he looked at Kennedy. Kennedy blushed so much it covered his neck. "I blew Peyton. God, Peyton's attractive."

"Peyton *is* attractive," Kennedy agreed.

"Do you remember anything after it?"

"No."

"Nothing?"

"No," I said, a bit warier. "What did I do?"

"Surprisingly nothing," Kennedy answered. He sounded proud and that made me feel good.

"Yes..." Theo said. "You didn't do anything, but I saw you talking to Devon at one point and I was dying to know what you guys talked about."

"Devon?" Kennedy and I said at the same time.

"Yes, our very own Princess Bitch."

Our very own Princess Bitch indeed. Devon had self-proclaimed himself the Princess of Ravenwood pretty much the same week Kennedy had become King, but unlike me, the self-proclaimed Queen, he had far less respect.

His respect grew moderately when he became Kennedy's boyfriend last year, and people started to actually warm to the self-proclaimed Princess Devon, because he was obviously in the King's good graces. That was until he very publicly broke up with Kennedy in some ridiculous plot to shame Kennedy's reign and take over. It hadn't worked obviously, and Kennedy had fallen in love with Stephen and they all lived happily ever after.

Whereas Devon was essentially cancelled, the choir where he resided disgraced. I tried to avoid him at all costs, throwing him a dirty look here and there to get my point across. I wouldn't have willingly spoken to him, about anything.

"I don't remember that at all."

"That's not good," Kennedy said, scrunching his nose at me. "Why did you get so drunk? You never get drunk..."

"No," I said, pointing at him. "I either get drunk or have sex, but I never get drunk *then* have sex."

"Just sometimes you have sex then get drunk," Theo said, and I smiled at him.

"Sometimes," I agreed.

"Cassidy?" Kennedy said.

"Father threatened to cut me off," I said. Kennedy frowned. "One more bill, and I'm cut off. I was pissed off, so I got drunk." I reached for my phone. There was a string of notifications, but that wasn't unusual.

I stopped scrolling when I saw a text from the contact affectionately named 'Not Cameron'.

Not Cameron: Up for a Sunday coffee?

I smiled, then I looked up between Kennedy and Theo.

"Is it still Saturday?" I asked.

Kennedy laughed as he stood from his bed. "Yes Cassidy, it's still Saturday," he replied.

"Musical auditions are this evening," Theo added. I swore.

I sat beside Finn on the fourth row in the stalls, taking the sheets he offered me after he was through reading them. Since Kennedy had become a royal and I'd proclaimed myself the real royal, Finn had requested I sit in the auditions with him, passing my judgement on the others. We both knew I was going to be the Squib; this had been officiated. But he wanted a second opinion on the rest of the class.

"I'm going to miss you next year," he said almost absently as he rifled through the headshots of the theatre boys. We got a new headshot every year, pre-audition, and they were used the entire year, in our programmes, in the wall displays for the musicals, for the auditions. He smiled affectionately at Archie when he got to him.

"I fully believe he'll be King at some point," I said, pointing at him.

"That'd be the day, one of my theatre Queens being King," he replied, and I smiled as he reached the picture of Oscar.

"With his King Consort?"

Finn gasped. "No way."

42

"Not officially," I said quickly.

Finn laughed then picked up the microphone that was settled next to him. "Theatre babies? Onto the stage please," he requested, and they came, standing in a big, long line from wing to wing. "To refresh your knowledge on auditioning, we will start with a group number, pre-selected I hope you've all already learnt, then we will work through your auditions. We will start with our darling first years. Everyone gets five minutes. Use it well.

"During your audition the rest of the theatre will be sat in the stalls, and I don't need to tell you fine young gentlemen to be respectful of each other, but I'm going to remind you anyway." He looked at me. "Anything to add?"

"No, I think you just about covered it. You're getting good at that," I said, and he smiled.

"Thank you, Queen," he said, then he turned towards the technician box. He waved, so I turned, smiling as Lewis in the box waved back. "Can I have our group number, please?"

"Course," Lewis replied, then pressed play. The room filled with the opening bars of 'One Day More'. Finn had given all the different voice types a different part in the song, and they sang through it perfectly.

Finn and I also sang it with them, Finn singing the male parts whilst I sang through the female, interspersed with giggles of laughter as we messed with each other.

We both applauded as the theatre boys left the stage and filled the stalls behind us. Finn pointed to the first, first year. I smiled a big smile that was intended to be comforting.

"John-Paul, you're up," he said, and JP stood, his hands wringing together before he made his way to the stage.

We sat by the fire doors, all the headshots between us on a chair as we worked our way through them whilst smoking a cigarette.

"What are we thinking?" Finn asked as I looked at Marley's headshot. I took the cigarette out of my mouth then shook my head.

"I don't know," I said, amused. "A lot. Who's playing the love interest?"

"Ah," he replied thoughtfully, then he shrugged. "If Theo's Michael, Marley could be Jeremy."

"Potentially."

"Then Lucah could be Christine, but Christian for our production."

"Good plan," I said.

He smiled as he smoked the end of the cigarette, leaning his head back to blow the smoke upwards. "Good work," he said, amused, then raised his hand so I high-fived him.

"I can come back next year..." I said. He frowned at me, shaking his head, but I cut him off quickly. "For auditions and things like that, I can come and help, and..."

"Cassidy, you'll be too busy living your life."

"I doubt it," I replied, and he sighed so I smiled at him. "We can make this work," I whispered. "We're good at that."

"True," he said, amused, as he collected the papers in front of me. "Still hungover?"

"Yes," I moaned.

He grinned. "So, you don't want to come back to my room?"

"Well, I never said that."

Five

Casper was waiting outside the coffee shop we'd agreed to meet at. He was leaning against the wall, headphones on, his phone in his hand.

I took a moment to look at him, finding amusement in the fact that I was blown away by just how much he looked like Cameron. He must've felt me hovering; he looked up then smiled at me, taking his headphones down and letting them hang around his neck.

We walked towards each other, standing and just looking at each other until we both began to laugh.

"You can shit-talk me, if it'll make it easier?" he said. I looked down, and he grinned.

"No," I said softly. He rose his eyebrow at me, so I smiled my Queen smile.

The smile I hid behind when the butterflies took off in my stomach. I wasn't sure why they were there; I didn't completely understand where this sudden nauseating nervousness had come from, but it was here and I wasn't too sure how to push it away.

Instead, I just smiled my Queen smile, all teeth and seductiveness, and I hid behind her because I knew how to do that best.

"Coffee?" he asked.

"Coffee," I agreed. He smiled as he opened the door, stepping back to let me through. I'm pretty sure I blushed so I lifted my scarf, covering my cheeks as I walked towards the barista. It was the same girl who'd written her 'a's as hearts the last time we were here.

We both got our coffee in a mug, then sat at a two-person table. I took a deep breath; he beat me to it.

"What were the auditions for?"

I frowned at him.

"You sent me a text last night. You said yes to this coffee, and sorry it took so long but you were at auditions."

"Oh! Our summer musical. My last musical, I guess. We were auditioning so we could get casting."

"You auditioned?"

"No, I oversaw them."

"Oh." He was teasing me; I could tell given the twinkle in his eye, the laugh in his expression. It made my heart trip over itself. "We just do a concert. We all have a solo piece and the younger years do group numbers to break it up."

"What are you going to perform?"

"I don't know, we get given a theme at some point."

"A theme?"

"Yeah, few years ago it was Disney. We've had musicals, pop songs. It can literally be anything."

"You play the trumpet, right?" I asked. He nodded as he drank from his coffee. "I love the trumpet. I mean, Kennedy plays the sax and it's beautiful; the sound it produces is something else. I could listen to him playing it all day, but I also *love* the trumpet. It's got such a rich sound." I paused. "Sorry."

"Sorry?" he repeated, sounding surprised. "Did you just apologise for showing passion about the thing I am *most* passionate about?"

"I guess I did," I replied, and he laughed into his coffee. We smiled at each other for a few minutes then I looked away.

"I love musicals, for the record," he said. "Cam and I used to go to a theatre group together. Now he just takes me to every and *any* musical he can."

"That sounds ideal," I said, amused. "Kennedy is *for* it. Loves musicals and always has, but now he has a boyfriend."

"I'll go to the theatre with you," he said softly. "Cam has a boyfriend, too." He drank from his coffee as I played with the mug. "I think I know Kennedy's boyfriend," he continued curiously, and I was thankful for him keeping the conversation going.

"You do?"

"Yeah, I was playing the match when there was that big dramatic love declaration."

"You're a Golden footballer, too. Oh, Casper you really have nothing going for you."

He laughed happily. "Hey, we had a winning streak. We won every…"

"I'll tell you right now, I don't care about football," I said.

A little piece of folded paper caught my eye as I opened my locker. I frowned at it, looking around the hallway then reaching for it. I unfolded it then smiled.

Enjoyed being with you this weekend. Let's do it again x

I refolded it on itself, looking around the hallway before slipping the note into my blazer. Finn wasn't usually so bold, or in fact one for love notes, and I doubted that Casper was able to make his way into the school to put a note into my locker. Unless he knew someone. Which wasn't too unlikely.

"Hey."

I jumped. I closed my locker quickly and looked at Theo as he leant on his locker. His eyes widened at me as I put on my mask, displaying calmness and composure, even if my heart was jack-rabbiting out my chest.

He laughed as his eyes trailed me. "Good?" he asked.

"Obviously. You?"

"I have an issue," he replied. I frowned at him as he sighed overdramatically. "Mum sent me a message this morning telling me that her and Dad had booked tickets to see *Dear Evan Hansen* tonight, but unfortunately they can't actually make it anymore." He sighed deeply as I hit his arm. "I said I couldn't *possibly* take the tickets, because who on Earth would I go with."

"If you did, we're not friends anymore."

He laughed. "Half seven. Stalls tickets."

"You are the *best*," I squeaked, then kissed his cheek. He laughed as the bell rang through the corridor. We both looked up towards the noise. "Have you seen Archie?" I asked.

He shook his head as he walked around me to walk down the corridor. "Not since the audition. How will you possibly live without your gossip?" he said in a gasp as we stopped outside of our Maths classroom. I shook my head as I looked down the corridor then stepped through the door.

"Hey," I said, walking towards the group of third years who were sat huddled in the stalls. They all sat up a little straighter, silencing their conversation as if they expected me to tell them off.

"Hey?" the most ballsy of the herd said. I think he was called Dante, but I couldn't be sure.

"Where's my darling Archie today?" I asked. Dante smiled as the second year who I knew was Oscar looked towards me, his eyes examining me.

"He's sick."

"Oh no," I replied. It may've sounded insincere even though that totally wasn't my intention. "How sick?"

"Woke up with a stuffy nose. He's feeling a bit sorry for himself, but Mr Henderson came to see him and said he should take the day off."

"Oh." I tutted. "Poor Archie." Finn clapped his hands, getting everyone's attention so he could excuse us. "Where do you guys live?" I asked. Dante frowned at me. "What?"

"Why do you want to know?"

"Archie," I said as if it was obvious, but Dante didn't seem impressed.

"He's the Queen, tell him," another hissed.

Dante rolled his eyes. "Scarlett corridor. Fifty-six."

"Are you his roommate?" I asked, and he nodded. "Good, I'll go with you then." He seemed even less impressed, then stood as Finn evacuated everyone with a bit more gusto. I waved to him, blowing him a kiss and making him laugh as I followed the little herd of whispering third years out of the theatre and towards the boarding house. Occasionally they looked back at me, with wide eyes and gaped mouths, none of them actually daring to speak to me. How I loved the younger years.

I remembered how much Kennedy and I had hero-worshipped King Ash, the boy who ruled before us. We hung on his every word. Followed him like he was Jesus reborn and we were his willing disciples.

We turned onto the Scarlett corridor and I couldn't help but laugh as many of the third years ran from room to room. Most of their doors were wide open and there were boys everywhere, because in third year boarding school still felt like one long sleepover. As I walked pass them they mostly stilled, their conversations dying because I was the Queen. I feared some may wet themselves if Kennedy were to walk these corridors.

Only the door with fifty-six on it was closed. Dante gestured to me, telling me that was in fact the door.

"I'm going for tea," he told me as he put his key into the door. He clicked the lock and I held the doorknob. "Tell Archie I'll bring him some soup."

I nodded, then pushed open the door. I was taken aback for a second by the smell of hormones. The ripeness of teenage boys right on the cusp of puberty. I wondered how rude it'd be perceived if I opened a window.

I smiled at Archie when I saw him, sat in his bed, a blanket wrapped around his shoulders, but sat above his duvet. He had a box of tissues in front of him, and some used tissues around him. He had baby blue joggers on, and a t-shirt that looked like a cluster of stars, a galaxy. He looked surprised to see me, and I couldn't blame him.

"I was worried," I said. "How am I meant to keep up on the daily news if my guy is sick?"

"Sorry," he replied, his voice weak, his nose blocked. I shook my head as he began to pick up his tissues. He hid them under the blanket.

"Don't be sorry, baby," I said as I sat on the end of his bed.

"I don't even have your daily update."

"Well, it's lucky I do then," I said. He frowned so I shrugged. "I kept myself in the loop. I wouldn't want you to miss a day."

He laughed, nodding to me. "Well go on, give me the low down. Last I knew Devon was being *weirdly* quiet. Kennedy and Stephen were reigning supreme."

"All of this is still true," I said, "but Rowan and Lucah are on a break."

"Really? But they were a total OTP."

"I know," I said, sounding just as shocked. "There's something else going on there for sure, but Rowan was being quiet. I thought for a little while that it had to do with Marley."

"No," Archie said, shaking his head, then he sniffed and groaned. I smiled as I handed him a tissue. He looked extremely grateful as he blew his nose. "Marley has his own thing going on."

"Really?"

"Yeah. He's definitely got *someone* but I don't know who."

"Letting the side down, Archie."

"Oh shut up, Queen," he said. I laughed, my fingers brushing the note in my blazer pocket. I frowned at him. "What?" he asked softly as I pulled the note out of my pocket.

"Do you happen to know who's handwriting this is?" I unfolded the note for him.

He took it, his eyebrow raising almost instantly as he read over the note. "Well, who did you spend the weekend with?" he asked as he ran his finger over the letters.

I laughed. "The entirety of my year, at Lucah's party on Friday, all you theatre babies at the auditions on Saturday…"

"Finn on Saturday night."

"Casper on Sunday."

"Casper?" he repeated, I waved my hand, "did you, you know, get with someone at the party?"

"Peyton." I said.

"He's beautiful," he said in a sigh, and I smiled. "It could be from him, he's the pianist, isn't he?" he asked. I nodded. "I would imagine pianists would have such beautiful handwriting."

"This is valid."

"Do you normally get notes thanking you for sex?"

"We didn't have sex," I replied as I took the note back. "I just blew him, and *no* I don't normally get thank you notes."

He giggled childishly. "Personally, I'd count a blowjob as sex," he said, then sneezed again, covering his face as he sighed.

"How are things with Oscar?" I asked.

He gasped then blushed brightly. "Good."

"Tell me more." I grinned as I crossed my legs on his bed.

He shook his head at me. "You'll catch a cold."

I shrugged, and he smiled right back.

Kennedy and I have an older brother. Who had a husband and three darling children of his own, and although they still lived in Brighton near to our family home, I tried to visit as often as I could – if only because baby Ryder was gorgeous, and I wanted to soak up all the baby time I could have with him. Dom, his husband, didn't mind and Harrison seemed to enjoy the company.

He worked for our father. I didn't really know the

54

details, but I did know I owed him a huge debt, because if he hadn't gone into the family business, that'd mean Father would've expected Kennedy or me to, and neither of us were made for politics.

Unless of course it was a production of *Hamilton*, then sign me up because I want to play Angelica Schuyler.

But Kennedy and I were made for the stage, both of us in equal measure, and because Harrison essentially distracted Father, we both got to do that.

That, and he was the eldest. Our father's firstborn and all that weird heir stuff.

He was thirty this year, a proper man having been the result of Father's first marriage.

Harrison's mum had died from a virus that, because she was HIV positive, had made her immune system weaker, and had in turn caused Harrison to be tested at age ten, to discover he too was HIV positive. Which was a lot for Harrison but apparently a lot for our poor father, who still believed HIV to be the *gay disease*.

It was a completely irrelevant fact Harrison was gay. Just because he had the two factors didn't mean they collated with each other, but that was a bit too much for our poor father's head to comprehend.

He had Kennedy and me to our mum, his second marriage, when Harrison was twelve and well enrolled in Ravenwood. We hardly saw him the first six years of our lives as he boarded, and when he left he went straight into work with Father.

"So, Father mentioned you were stealing money from

him…" he said absently as he shrugged off his blazer and gasped happily at Ryder, who was pushing himself off the floor to toddle towards his daddy.

"I don't know what you're referring to," I told him; Harrison laughed dramatically as he picked Ryder up, blowing raspberries onto his hands.

"He'll kill you, you know. He knows people."

"Of that I have no doubt," I told him, and he laughed. "I'm *not* stealing, I'm simply borrowing."

"Why, when you have an allowance?"

"You're starting to sound like him, Harrison. It isn't a good look."

He rolled his eyes at Ryder who giggled, throwing his whole little body at Harrison.

"He means…"

"Don't say well; don't tell me he means well."

"You might see it if you stop squeezing money out of him," he said. I looked away from him as he put Ryder back onto the floor. He toddled back to me, clapping his hands when he reached me. I grinned, clapping back.

"He's got enough of it."

"That may be true."

I sighed; he also did, taking his tie off then his jacket before sitting in front of me.

"Where's Kennedy?" he asked as Ryder looked between us, obviously conflicted about who he wanted to sit with.

"Stephen," I muttered. He tapped his foot against mine.

"Hey…"

"They're on a date, I don't know where."

"So you came to see your brother?"

"I came to see Ryder," I told him. "And Dom, I like Dom."

"Where *is* Dom?"

"He's upstairs. Millie was pretty serious about her tea party."

"Always is… where's Wesley?"

"Xbox."

He looked up towards the stairs, nodding slowly as if it made perfect sense.

"You'll find *someone* you know…" he said, obviously warily as he refused to look at me. I laughed and it came out as a pretty unattractive squawk. It made Ryder jump. "Cass…"

"I have *plenty* of people," I told him, because I *did*.

I had Theo, and Archie, and Marley – whenever I wanted, I had Marley in fact. Most of the theatre boys and even some of the choir boys. All at my beck and call. I even had Finn. Most of the time.

"I mean…"

"I *know* what you mean. I am *fully* aware what you mean, but I don't want that, I don't want a boyfriend or a relationship. I don't want to be monogamous or whatever."

"Okay," he said.

"Okay," I snapped back; he lifted his hand.

"Okay."

"*Okay*."

Six

"I love it here," Casper told me as we walked through Trafalgar Square. "London. Like, London as a whole, not just here." He smiled shyly as he took a sip from the cup that had *Cassie* written on it, because I *knew* the barista couldn't hear me, especially given the confused AF look she'd given me when I said the name required on the two coffees.

Casper had laughed and laughed and told me he understood more than anyone could, and we'd continued to laugh as we started walking, telling each other all the mistaken names we got on a regular basis.

Casey, and Katie, and Cat, and of course Jasper.

We'd ended up walking to Trafalgar Square, and towards the fountains.

"You're not from London?"

"You think I'm from here?" he said in a laugh. I watched him as he continued towards the fountains, reaching his hand out to touch the water as it crashed down the tiers.

"Where are you from?"

"Guess?" he almost whispered, his expression playful. I sat beside him on the fountain even though it was the end of February, and still far too cold for that kind of thing.

"The North?" I guessed, and he hummed at me as he nodded. "Speak for me again."

He pressed his lips together tightly, shaking his head at me, so I smiled, looking down, playing with the plastic of my coffee cup.

"You're not from Scotland," I told him.

"No," he laughed.

"Manchester."

"Oh, *higher*." He pointed up as I frowned at him thoughtfully.

"Liverpool."

"Close," he whispered. I examined him. "Smaller, but still thriving…" he said. "Las Vegas's second cousin, a few times removed…"

"Blackpool," I said, laughing. He grinned at me, nodding. "Wait, so how did you end up in a London school?"

"Scholarship," he replied, then he turned to me, sitting crossed legged, his coffee in front of him. "When Cam and I were almost eleven we went to Goldstein's summer camp, two weeks at the beginning of the summer. Musical theatre mostly; you get a taster of all their classes, then spend the second week putting together a production, which you perform on the Friday before you go home.

"We both loved every second of it and, well, I guess we were both good because by the end of the camp Goldstein offered us both scholarships for the Musical Theatre course. There were stipulations, of course.

"We had to pass the first year, you know the usual kind of terms and conditions, but I said I didn't want to do theatre, as much as I loved it."

"But Cameron said yes?"

"Yeah. He was well up for it, and loves every second of it. There's no regrets there. When induction day came around we all drove up of course, but the school had requested I bring my trumpet because I'd mentioned it during the camp."

"And Goldstein's a music school, too."

"Exactly. Two campuses, Music and Theatre. The only time the two campuses even see each other is the last show put on in seventh year, when we're the orchestra for the musical."

"You auditioned, I assume?"

"They asked me to play something for them, *anything*. I was only eleven. I played 'All That Jazz', because I panicked and figured they wanted a musical song, but they were impressed, I guess, because they gave me a full scholarship to the Music course. Unlike Cam who only got his first year paid for. I had to choose Musical Theatre as my final project which I was probably going to anyway."

"That's amazing," I told him, and he smiled. "I don't

know if I could be without Kennedy though; having him on a different campus would be terrible."

"Terrible?" he repeated.

I nodded. "He's my twin."

"Cam's mine," he said, grinning at me. "We've always been separated though: different classes in little school; I went to music lessons, he *didn't*. How did you two end up in Ravenwood then?"

"Our father's a benefactor," I said, shrugging.

"Oh, you're a rich kid," he whispered. I laughed. "And head of the theatre?"

"Of course. I *am* the Queen."

"The *Queen*?" he repeated.

"Yeah, Kennedy's the King, therefore *I* am the Queen."

"Oh."

"Oh?"

He looked up at me, shaking his head slowly. "I just thought you meant something else. It's *okay*."

"Casper?"

"I've only just figured out I'm… bi. I guess."

"Really?" I said quietly.

He nodded again. "Pan; I'm pan. I kind of denied it for a while. I mean, Cameron's gay. He's been out since he was like twelve, so I figured I couldn't be, but I definitely like boys and have *always* definitely liked boys. I just haven't really admitted to it," he sighed. "We don't know each other very well. It's probably not time for *this* conversation."

"Casper."

"I think I'm nonbinary," he said, then glanced at me. "Which doesn't really call for why I didn't admit to liking boys, but whatever. I think I'm nonbinary."

"And you thought because I said I was the Queen…"

"Yeah."

"I mean, I've never really thought about it," I said quietly. "I'm definitely not conforming; anyone who knows me can confirm that. I mean straight off the bat…"

"You call yourself the Queen," he said softly.

"I do…" I said, amused, then, "I've been calling you he, is that right?"

"Yeah, he, him is right… I think. I don't know, it's a bit complicated trying to figure out your gender in an all-boys' school."

And it was, he was right. Sure, the boys in my school just looked at me in a dress and expected that of me. They usually cheered me on, but I figured if someone else did it there'd be whispers behind hands and side glances.

"Your friends?"

"They're awesome," he replied. "My best friend, Nick, he's the drummer, he's really supportive and awesome."

"Good," I said, grinning at him as he laughed, shaking his head.

"That got deep *real* quick…" He cleared his throat. "Your favourite musical is?"

"Oh," I said. He laughed. "Oh that's tough, it's between three."

"Okay?" He lifted up three fingers. I grinned, touching the first one.

"*Everybody's Talking about Jamie…*" I said. "*Dear Evan Hansen.*"

"Of course," he said, nodding as I touched his middle finger. "And my last one is between *Heathers* and *Six*. I just I cannot choose between my Queens."

"That is fair," he said.

I laughed then turned away from him to sneeze. I smiled at him as he held a tissue out to me. "Thank you," I said, hiding behind the tissue as I shook my head. "What is yours?"

"My favourite musical?" he asked. "*Be More Chill.*"

I wiped my nose. "Really?"

He nodded, almost frowning at me, but that was probably because I had replied quite perkily.

"That's our summer show. I'm the Squib."

"That's *perfect.*"

"You can come see it, if you want," I suggested. He began to nod. I sneezed again. "*Oh,*" I moaned

"You're not getting sick, are you?"

"No," I answered. "I hope not," I groaned, rubbing my forehead. "Oh, I hope not."

I *was* getting sick. I woke up Monday morning and everything felt heavy. My nose felt stuffy, my throat scratchy. I tried to stay in bed.

"Lessons start in ten, Cass," Kennedy told me, shaking my shoulders. I tried to bat him away.

"I'm sick."

"You just don't like Maths," Theo said, laughing. I lowered my duvet to look at him as he grinned at me whilst tying his tie.

"I mean, sure," I murmured as Kennedy rolled his eyes. I groaned, lifting the duvet back over my head.

"I'll see you later," he said. I heard the door open. I lowered the duvet again. Cody smirked at me as he buttoned up his shirt. He sat on my bed.

"You're really sick, huh," he said.

"You believe me?"

He nodded softly, stroking my hair out of my face. "You're far more dramatic when you're pretending you're sick."

I laughed as he grinned at me.

"I'll get you some soup at lunch, and bring it back for you," he added.

"Thank you," I muttered.

"Rest up, Queen," he said as he stood from my bed. I blew a kiss to him.

"Cody…" I said softly. He turned back to look at me as he pulled his tie off his bed. "Nose ring." . He pointed at me, twisting the little ring up and out of sight.

"Thank you, darling, see you at lunch time."

He left the room.

I tried to go back to sleep, but I couldn't because I was so awake. I was stuffy and my head hurt and I wanted to chop my nose off, but I wasn't tired at all, so I put on a hoodie, a big hoodie that I *think* belonged to Marley, or Cody, or maybe Kennedy – possibly Finn. I stepped into my sleep shorts, and Chucks, then left our room.

The hallways were deserted as I expected them to be. The bell had rang through, herding everyone into class. It was weird, the corridors being so empty, so quiet. I went to my locker.

There was a note poking out of it.

Like I expected.

My Queen, so what are we? A secret? A game? Needless to say it's been a lot of fun. I look forward to seeing you this week already. Maybe a date sometime soon? What do you think about that? X

Weird. Really weird. I put it in my pocket, continuing down the deserted corridor until I reached the theatre. The door was loud when I opened it. Finn jumped out of his skin.

"Oh my god, Cassidy," he said, turning to look at me, his hand on his chest. I waved as I pushed the door closed behind me. "Shouldn't you be in class?"

"I'm sick."

"Ew," he said. I laughed then sneezed; it, in fact, *was* ew. I walked down the stalls, my fingers stroking over the note in my pocket. I stopped at the end of the row he was sat on. He looked at me, his eyes scanning me, then he bit his lip.

"You really are sick, huh," he commented. I rounded my eyes at him. "Come here," he added, his voice overly sympathetic. I laughed but went to sit next to him.

His eyes roamed over me, then his hand was against

my forehead. His expression genuinely became concerned.

"You *are* sick."

"Why doesn't anyone *actually* believe me?"

"You're a drama queen," he told me. I mocked him and he mocked me straight back. "How did you get sick?"

"I'm going to blame Archie," I said. "I love the kid but yeah he definitely got me sick."

"Oh, not our heir," he said dramatically. I laughed as I looked over his little makeshift table. He was annotating the script ready for Saturday rehearsals to begin this week, and I fully appreciated how he highlighted every theatre boy a different colour. "You can stay here, but I do have to do work."

"Wait, you *work* here?" I asked. He looked at me so I grinned.

"I have Second Year after break."

I groaned. He smirked as he continued to annotate the script. I watched as he wrote, pulling the note out of my pocket.

It wasn't *his* handwriting. I mean, I'd have hoped I'd have recognised his handwriting if it was Finn's, but it *not* being his made me nervous.

Which was stupid, right? Because I was the Queen; I shouldn't be nervous at a note, but on the other hand I was the Queen and that meant I could be on anybody's shit list.

"You're not here today, are you?" Finn whispered. I hummed back at him. "Hey," he said lifting my chin. I blinked a few times.

"Oh, what?"

You're lost in your head aren't you?" he said, stroking back my hair. "Or are you just really sick?"

"I *am* dying," I told him, and he laughed as his eyes scanned the theatre. They obviously found what they were looking for – which turned out to be nothing – as he kissed my forehead. I whimpered as he lifted my chin.

"I'm not going to kiss you properly, you're dying."

"I'm… okay," I said. "I'll be back on my throne tomorrow."

"I'm sure," he whispered. "You're icky though. Look at you."

"You bitch," I replied, and he winked at me before turning towards the door as the bell rang.

"I'll see you tomorrow. Okay? Bright eyed, bushy tailed, and not dripping from your nose."

"Oh," I groaned, covering my nose.

He smiled, passing me a tissue. "Go rest up, darling."

I was sat on our windowsill that overlooked the wooded area behind the school. It was closed off now; you couldn't stray too far into the trees. The furthest Kennedy and I got was to a manmade campfire circle which was just far enough away that we could smoke weed and not get caught by the smell ratting us out.

Harrison used to go further. I'd seen pictures of him and his friends deep in the woods because that's where they hung out, the four of them, him and Preston and their two other friends, identical twins. They'd climb trees and sit up amongst the treetops. The school had closed it off not long after Preston had died, as that was where they'd found him.

I barely jumped when Cody sat opposite me on the windowsill, stripping himself of his blazer and passing me a polystyrene bowl of soup.

"Chicken and sweetcorn," he told me, before adding, "it's nice." I smiled as I popped the lid off the bowl and began to sip from it. "What are you thinking about?"

"The woods," I said, and we both looked out the window together. "Preston."

"Hey," he said softly. I looked back at him. "I know you're sick and everything but…"

"I'm not thinking about him like that," I said, shaking my head. "I just can't believe we leave this place in, what, five months? Just like that, seven years…" I clicked my fingers. "And it's over in five months."

"You get philosophical when you're sick, huh…" He smiled at me. "I thought it was just weed that made you go like that."

I grinned at him over the soup. "Thank you for the soup."

"Feeling better?"

"A little," I said, then cleared my throat. "I plan on sleeping all afternoon." I paused. "If that fails, I downloaded a new audio book."

"I like soft Cassidy."

"*Soft* Cassidy?"

"Yeah. Sat in a big hoodie, relaxed, hair not immaculate, listening to audiobooks and speaking softly, not biting or bitching or…" He shrugged. "I like soft Cassidy."

"Cody…" I said. "Why did we sleep together only once?"

"This is the question, Cass," he said, nodding. I laughed. "Kennedy still doesn't know and as his best friend I feel like I should tell him that we had sex."

I waved my hand at him. "Unless you want to get serious," I said, then winked at him. He laughed.

"I'm good," he told me. I drank more soup. "No offence."

"None taken, baby doll, none taken." I smiled at him. "I didn't know there was a soft Cassidy though, that's enlightening."

He laughed happily as he looked back out of the window. "We don't see him a lot," he said, nodding. "I like him. He held my hand during this," he said, pointing to his nose. I gasped.

"You held my hand during that…" I told him, twisting the piercing on my nipple. I gasped lightly as he laughed.

"That was a good day," he said. "Hysterical, and poor Kennedy."

"He felt so left out," I said, "and then he tried to team up with Theo."

"Who couldn't talk because of his tongue," he laughed. I grinned at him.

"He'd never have gotten anything pierced anyway, he's too much of a wimp."

"Stephen would, though."

"Stephen definitely would," I said, laughing. "I like Stephen."

"I *love* Stephen," he said, smiling. "He's perfect for Kennedy."

I turned as my phone buzzed on my bedside table. We both frowned at it as I stood from the windowsill, walking towards it then grinning stupidly at *Not Cameron* on my screen.

"Oh, that's an I-want-to-sleep-with-you smile." He grinned. I turned quickly to look at him as he smirked at me, shrugging his blazer back on and turning his nose ring so it was hidden.

"You don't know what you're talking about."

"Oh, I do. I've smiled at many boys like that. Who is it?"

"Not your business," I replied.

"I hear you, I hear you," he said softly, then he kissed my cheek. "Get better, Queen, so you can get your fuck."

I pushed him away by the shoulder.

"Shut up," I said, laughing as I sat back on my bed. He winked at me as he left our room. I unlocked my phone.

Not Cameron: Just gone on lunch. I'd pander to you, and ask if you were okay, but you're the QUEEN so, buck up 😬

Cassidy: How long do you have for lunch?

Not Cameron: 1 hour!

Not Cameron: So, I'm all yours for the next sixty minutes.
Not Cameron: Well, fifty-six minutes.

Cassidy: 😁 🫶

I walked down the corridor with Theo, our arms linked as we navigated the deserted Saturday morning corridor. Pyjama Rehearsals were something of Finn's creation as he figured if he had to get up on a Saturday morning to run a rehearsal, and we had to get up to be at said rehearsal, that we all might as well do it in the comfort of our pyjamas.

When I was in third year, the sevenths at that point thought it'd be hilarious if we all turned up in the same pyjamas – and, all things considered, it was hilarious, or at least Finn's reaction was. Now, as it was tradition, I teased Finn with a suggestion that we all just come in dressing gowns.

He'd growled at me, saying I wouldn't dare, and I really considered… daring, especially when he threatened me with what he'd do if I did dare. In the end, I'd sent a link to everyone with a very simple dark blue pair of long pyjamas with baby blue stars that glowed in the dark. I was very much looking forward to the blackouts between scenes.

We were the first in the theatre, but that wasn't unexpected. Theo and I were usually the first to arrive. Finn turned towards us, smiling at us as we walked in, and I grinned back because since it had become tradition Finn had insisted on always wearing the same pyjamas, and he was.

He turned, leaning against his table, crossing his arms over his chest as we walked towards him. Theo walked past towards the stage as I leant on the seating bank. His eyes roamed me and I let them, resting my arms on the seating bank behind me, smiling with him when he reached my feet and my white hi-top Chuck Taylors. I looked him up and down, amused at his choice of white trainers.

"Do you have anywhere to be this afternoon?" he asked. I shook my head slowly as I played with the nearest seat to me. "Not at all?"

"Not after rehearsal finishes, no. The King is attending the football game to spare me."

"Ah, of course, the football game," he said. "How convenient."

"Smooth," I whispered.

"You'd think I planned these things, but I genuinely don't," he said, nodding to me. "I'm innocent in all this."

"You're never innocent," I said, then I groaned because I wanted to kiss him. I wanted to move into him and place a soft kiss on his lips, a fleeting thing, full of love and without consequence, but I couldn't and my palms itched with how much I wanted to touch him. He smiled, reaching out for me so our fingers touched. He locked our fingers around each other, pulling my hand to his lips and lightly kissing them.

"Later," he said, then winked. "I do hope you have

your script, Queen."

"Ha," I said as I walked around him. "I don't need my script." I climbed onto the stage and stood beside Theo. The door to the theatre opened. Archie leant against it as the other third years walked through it. "Looking good, Arthur," I called. He laughed, smiling at me so I grinned back.

"Feeling better, Queen?" he asked.

I nodded to him, touching my chest. "It was touch and go for a while," I said. "We almost had a day off."

"What?" Finn said, laughing as he jumped up onto the stage, sitting on the edge and turning to look at me.

"You get a day off if the Queen dies."

"Oh," he said.

"Oh my god," Theo laughed. "You're so dramatic. It was a cold," he stated. I turned to him. He rose his hands. "A killer cold."

"Exactly."

"I told you you'd get sick," Archie said as he joined us on the stage. "I told you."

"No one likes a know it all," I sung, wrapping my arms around him. He laughed, cuddling me back, looking up at me so I kissed him.

He blushed red, burying his head between us, so I cuddled him tighter.

"Take a seat, we'll do a read through first, then a sing through." I let go of Archie, his cheeks still red as he sat beside his friends. I sat next to Finn, our knees knocking together as I sat cross-legged. He glanced at me as he leant his script on his other raised knee.

"Hi," I whispered; he rolled his eyes, amused, before kneeing me lightly.

"Act one, scene one. We open with Jeremy…" he read. We all looked towards Marley as he began to read.

Finn ordered pizza to the theatre for our lunch – even though the canteen was of course still open, he told us that he felt we deserved pizza for rehearsing through our Saturday. He sent Theo and me for the pizza, as he trusted us the most to bring *all* the pizza back.

We started towards the door before we'd had the notification to tell us it was arriving, walking the empty corridors. We passed our lockers.

I stopped at mine. It was littered with get well notes because, apparently, I was rumoured far sicker than I *actually* was, but it was there. What I was looking for.

The little corner of paper sticking out between the grates of my locker. I pulled on it, putting it between my hip and waistband, then I ran to catch up with Theo, running past him and spinning him around. He laughed as we turned the corner and walked out the front door.

The football team were training in the nearest cage, well within view of us as they did their sprints. The tennis team were playing rallies in the one behind them as the sports teams could only train on Saturdays. I turned when one of the cages rattled.

"Hey!" Stephen shouted as he took deep breaths. We both ran towards him. "What are you doing?"

"Waiting for pizza," Theo answered.

Stephen groaned, resting his head on the cage.

"That's not fair. Why are you wearing pyjamas?"

"Pyjama rehearsal," Theo said, laughing as I reached for the note. I turned away from them, looking at the front gates as I unfolded the note.

Heard you've been sick. Consider this a get well note. Get well soon, Queen, as I want to go on a date with you at some point. Our little secret xoxo

Seven

The 'Brothers' group chat was *alive*.

Harrison: Gala, Saturday. Dad said it's really important that we're all there and looking our best. Car will come and pick you guys up around 1pm.

The King: Gala for what?

Harrison: Can't say...

The King: Because you don't know?

Harrison: No because I can't say...

    Cassidy: because he doesn't know x
    Cassidy: are we getting beautified? Will I need to shave and shower prior to this? x

Harrison: I do know.

The King: He doesn't

    Cassidy: so doesn't. x
    Cassidy: ANSWER my beautified question. X

Harrison: YES! You'll get beautified. Dad said no makeup.

    Cassidy: that's a bold decision he's making there with how he's aging…

Harrison: Cassidy

    Cassidy: no makeup.

Kennedy laughed beside me, so I looked at him as he bit his thumb nail.

"You know wearing makeup makes him nervous."

"I know he's a poor specimen of a man," I said.

Kennedy laughed. "Let's upset Harrison further."

The King: Can I bring Stephen?

I laughed; Kennedy grinned.

Harrison: Dad asked in what capitcy?
Harrison: capaticity*
Harrison: capatity*

      Cassidy: capacity

Harrison: Thank you.

The King: Boyfriend capacity. Obviously.

Harrison is typing…

We looked at each other, him grinning at me then at Cody as he climbed onto the end of Kennedy's bed, his homework folder between his knees.

Harrison: Dad said he can come if you guys don't let on that you're boyfriends.

      Cassidy: for real…

The King: and you're okay with that?

Harrison: Course not, but…

"You know what Father's like," Kennedy and I said out loud. Cody looked between us.

"Oh dear," he said quietly, as Kennedy dropped his phone onto his bed then sat forward so he could read what Cody had brought to his bed. "What's going on?"

"Gala," I murmured.

"Not Friday night?" he asked. We both looked up at him.

"Why? What's Friday night?"

"Spring Fling," he answered, then rolled his eyes. "Or whatever it is that Marley and Lucah are calling it this year."

"Party?" I asked. Cody nodded. "No, not Friday. We can do both, *right?*"

"We can do both," Kennedy agreed, then looked towards his phone as it vibrated. He smirked slightly.

"Stephen," Cody and I said together.

"Can you get some weed for the party?" Cody asked as he shook his head in Kennedy's direction.

"I can see what I can do. For you…" I added, and he touched his chest.

"You're the best."

"I know," I whispered.

Casper laughed as I rested him courtesy of my phone screen on the sink between the taps. I took a few steps back, stroking over my chin to make sure I'd shaved close enough before raising my arms and twirling.

"You look gorgeous," he told me. I turned to smile at him, looking down before clearing my throat, because the *Queen* did not blush and act coy. My outfit was simple really, just a shirt and jeans, but my shirt was half pastel pink, half yellow, a pastel blue collar and pocket tucked into my stonewash ripped jeans and my white trainers – but he couldn't quite see them.

"Thanks," I said softly. He laughed then turned his head, shushing someone. "Who are you with?" I asked, standing on my tiptoes as if that would let me see further into his room.

"Just Nick," he said, rolling his eyes.

Nick scoffed. "*Just*," he said, sounding scandalised. Casper rolled his eyes again before turning his phone. I lost my breath, touching my chest.

"You're gorgeous," I told Nick, because I felt like gorgeous people deserved to be told that fact. He blushed, shaking his head at me.

"Shush, Queen," he said sheepishly.

I laughed as Casper gasped. "Excuse me, you're supposed to be flirting with me."

"Oh baby, I *am* flirting with you, don't you worry."

"*And* he has a boyfriend," Casper said accusingly. Nick smirked at me.

"Lucky guy," I said, nodding.

"You might know him," Casper said, turning the camera back to his face. It was far too close which he noticed quite quickly, and covered his face until it was a safe distance away.

"Who is this lucky, *lucky* guy?"

"Thomas," Nick said off-screen.

"Thomas McNally?"

"For real?" I asked. Casper nodded, long slow nods. "Wow."

"You do know him?"

"Course, the theatre school blogs are a buzz with him, Harley Railton, and Justin…"

"Justin Prince," Casper said with a slight snarl.

"The talent, and the beauty, quite the couple," I said. Nick laughed as Casper frowned at me. "What? I'm talking about us."

He looked away from the screen. I laughed as I put my makeup bag on the edge of the sink. I glanced down at Casper, watching as he hit an off-screen Nick before I looked back in the mirror to put on my eyeliner.

"What are your plans for the night?"

"Minimal," he said to me. I almost laughed. "Nick has some beer, and because his boyfriend is currently in *Book of Mormon* he has no excuse to abandon me."

"Not abandoning," Nick sang off-screen. I smiled as I looked back at the camera.

"If your popular kid party gets boring though, you can call me," he said cheerfully. I heard Nick's dramatic whine.

"Noted," I told him as I looked back into the mirror again. "I was…" I cleared my throat as I looked through my makeup bag. "I was thinking about what you said to me…" I fiddled with my lip-gloss. "… About being nonbinary."

"Oh?" he said. I nodded, meeting his eyes again.

"It was… *interesting*," I added, then cleared my throat.

"Interesting, right?" he said softly, so I sighed.

"When did you figure it out?" I asked.

"Still figuring," he laughed. "I mean, it makes sense.

81

Right now, the word nonbinary fits the best and feels the most comfortable, which I think is all it needs to do."

"Fit?" I asked.

"Fit," he said. "As I said the first time we talked about this, it's hard and it's *hard* being in an all-boys' school especially, and a twin."

"I relate," I said, looking towards the bathroom door at the raucous laughter that came from the other side.

"Do some late-night googling," he said. I frowned at him. "Look for definitions and work from there, look at nonbinary, and gender fluid. Look at genderqueer if one of them fits. Dig deeper."

"That's a good idea," I said, and he smiled.

"Text me too, whilst you're doing this text me, but it doesn't even have to relate to what you're reading, it can be random questions about musicals or memes, or telling me about how drunk you got at the party or who you hooked up with," he said with a laugh. "But text me."

"I'm going to get high, not drunk," I told him. "I will *not* be hooking up with anyone," I added. "I will text you."

We smiled at the same time then both jumped when there was a knock on the bathroom door.

"Cass..."

"Theo," I said softly, then opened the bathroom door. He smiled at me as he stepped past me then he stopped.

"Oh," he said as Casper waved at him. "I need to pee. I didn't realise you were on a call."

"It's okay," Casper said. "I've got to let the Queen

82

get ready for her subjects." I glanced at Theo as he grinned. "Text me, Cassidy."

"I will, Casper," I said softly as I picked up my phone. He waved, so I waved back then glanced at Theo as the call dropped.

"Who's Casper?" Theo asked as I closed the bathroom door behind me, leaning on it as Theo went to the toilet.

"I don't really know yet," I answered.

He looked at me as I shook my head. "That sounds serious."

"Complicated."

"Yeah?" he asked. I nodded, going back to the sink and putting my lip gloss on. I turned him by the shoulder when he came to wash his hands, putting the lip gloss on him too. "Where did you find him?"

"A coffee shop," I whispered; Theo smiled. "I mistook him for his brother, and *he* mistook *me* for Kennedy."

"That sounds like the beginning of a Fanfiction," he said. I laughed as he took my hands, holding them out in front of me so he could see my entire outfit. "You look beautiful."

"Says you," I told him. "This may be my favourite outfit of yours."

"I like spring," he said. "It means pastels and flowers and being unapologetic. I was going to wear this, but I think it'll pull yours together far better," he told me, going into his pocket, pulling out a chain with a daisy hanging from it. I smiled at him as he dropped it over my head, the daisy resting against my chest.

"Perfect," we whispered together then turned as the bathroom door opened. Cody swung on it, and his eyebrow raised in our direction.

"How much longer are you going to be?" he asked as I let my eyes trail him.

"We'll be right out," I told him. He saluted, letting the door close back over. I glanced back at Theo who nodded to me.

"Let's do this, Queen."

I nodded to him, kissing him softly before leaving the bathroom. My eyes rested on Kennedy first, then I tutted.

"You could've made an effort."

The apparent Spring Fling was held in Marley's house. The house that belonged to his lawyer mother rather than his lecturer father, as she was more likely to be otherwise occupied and not in the house. *Not* that we had such raucous parties that Angela's presence would cause us a disruption.

I sat on the sweeping staircase, a cup full of Coke in my hand because we didn't drink if we were going to get high; we didn't think it wise. I didn't know where Theo had gone. He'd disappeared quite sleekly to the point I hadn't even noticed he'd left my side. The party was soft, more a sit-in than a rave. Boys sat everywhere around the house talking, laughing and drinking. Sam Smith was playing out of speakers in the lounge, their latest song low and easy to listen to.

There were two boys sat in front of me a few steps down, totally enamoured with each other's mouths, their hands at risk of disappearing.

"Here."

I didn't jump, but I did turn as Rowan sat on the step below me, looking up at me, holding a cup.

I frowned at it. "What is it?"

"Coke," he answered. "*Diet* Coke. I noticed you were drinking soft."

"Thank you…" I said softly, watching as he placed the cup on the step next to me. "What are you after? My weed?"

"No," he said in a laugh. "A kiss." He shrugged. "Sex."

"No," I said softly. He frowned up at me.

"What's wrong, Queen?" he asked. I laughed and it almost came out as a bark. "You're not one to turn someone down."

"Did you just call me a slut? Because, spoiler alert, that isn't going to get me into bed."

"No…" he said slowly, carefully. "I'm not slut shaming you, Her Majesty."

"No, but you are taking the piss."

"Of course," he said, laughing. I smiled as I drank from my cup. "Why not?" He looked away from me and down towards the couple who I'm pretty sure were now sucking out each other's fillings. He pulled a face. I laughed.

"Why not?" I repeated,. "Why not, what?"

"Why won't you sleep with me? I'm exactly your

type."

"What, willing?" I said. He sighed. "You love Lucah."

"Lucah's a dick," he said but he wasn't committing fully to it. He sighed as he looked into his drink.

"Really?"

"Yes," he said simply. I rose an eyebrow at him, so he looked up at me.

"What did Lucah do?"

He mumbled something back to me. When I didn't reply he looked up at me.

"Doesn't matter."

"You're on a break for something that doesn't matter?"

"I didn't come to you for therapy."

"No, you're just lucky I'm feeling therapeutic," I told him; he quirked a smile. "Go to Lucah, Rowan. I'm not who you want in your bed tonight, and sleeping with me will only anger Lucah."

"We're on a break."

"Yeah, I've heard *that* before," I said, and he sighed.

"Should've come for weed."

"I'd have given you some," I said. He laughed. "Lucah will be with Marley, go find him."

"No. Marley's having sex with…" He looked up at me.

"With?"

"I don't know… someone."

"Rowan."

"I *don't* know," he stressed then cleared his throat. "Lucah won't be with him though, I can tell you that for sure."

"Spill."

"No," he said in a laugh, so I pushed him and he hit the banister. It shook as he held onto it and laughed more. "No, no I shouldn't have said anything," he said, pushing me back. I laughed, holding my drink up so it wouldn't spill.

"If I guess, will you tell me?"

"I'm not playing that game with you," he said, then he stood. "No way, Lucah will kill me and I'm already having to grovel for this stupid thing I did." I smirked. He shook his head at me then kissed my cheek.

"If you were single, I'd have said yes," I told him as he started up the stairs, "just so you know." He grinned before disappearing off down the corridor of bedrooms. I watched him go.

"Hey, gorgeous."

"Cody," I said as he stood on the other side of the stairs, leaning on the slope.

"You look lonely."

"I am not lonely; I am merely enjoying being alone."

"Oh," he said then shrugged. "I was going to offer you sex then weed," he said. I bit my lip. "But if you're enjoying being alone, I'm sure I could find someone else..."

"Why are you offering sex?"

"When you were sick, and asked me why we'd only had sex once, it got me thinking, and I wanted to change that. Participation optional, of course."

"Course," I repeated, amused, then stood from the

step. "Well, come on then," I said softly, starting up the stairs. He'd caught up with me by the time I got to the top. He grabbed my hand and spun me in a circle towards one of the many bedrooms. He pushed me up against the door as he closed it, smirking at me, his eyes looking all around me, so I kissed him, holding his chin in my hand. I pushed him away when he tried to add tongue. I shook my head at him, and he frowned.

"Cassidy..." he said.

I licked my lips, smirking as he followed my tongue around my lips. "Kneel before the Queen," I requested of him. He laughed and it sounded choked, but he did as I requested.

Of course.

He smirked up at me as he opened my pants, winking at me before swallowing me whole. Like I knew he would – and could.

I wasn't one really for receiving head, as I'd encountered far, far too many boys who had no idea how to do it properly – if any at all. Far too many of them thought just getting on their knees and putting a dick in their mouth constituted as a blowjob.

It obviously did *not* and I preferred to deliver such foreplay after extensive research late one night with Kennedy, and Cody, and Theo. All of us crowded around Cody's laptop and Theo's tablet, watching porn on one and reading numerous sex advice articles on the other. It had worked.

All trialled and tested and was proven to give us *all* a certain level of power over who we were giving said head too. Except in this situation, because we both knew I was in control even though he was the one on his knees.

Although I suppose he had a *little* bit of power knowing he – and sure, Theo – was the only person I'd allow in this position.

"Are you going to take it…?" I gasped, my head connecting with the door behind me as my fingers splayed in his hair. I felt him nod, so I laughed, closing my eyes, leaning my head back against the door, relishing how he didn't choke.

"*Fuck*," I whispered. He laughed, sitting back on his ankles, looking up at me as he wiped the back of his hand across his mouth. He quirked an eyebrow at me so I beckoned him up, kissing him when I could reach him.

He grinned at me, spinning me before pushing me back onto the bed.

I sat, pleasantly high, in Marley's garden. Theo was sharing the swinging seat with me, my legs over his thighs as he kept the swing moving back and forth. Marley was sat against the side of the seat, having somehow bribed his way into getting a shot of the weed.

Kennedy was sat on the garden chair next to us, Stephen on his knee, his head on Kennedy's shoulder, them talking quietly to each other, both also high. Cody too sat on the floor cross-legged making daisy chains.

I took the opportunity of the quiet.

Cassidy: some interesting reading…

Not Cameron: Party that bad that you're googling nonbinary terms, huh? Popular kids parties not all they're cracked up to be.

> **Cassidy**: Shhhhhh
> **Cassidy**: we're high. It's great. Good weed. Have you ever smoked weed? I recommend it. Only good weed though.

Not Cameron: Come back to me Queen.

> **Cassidy**: I like the genderqueer flag.

Not Cameron: Just the flag?

> **Cassidy**: The description too.
> **Cassidy**: it made sense.
> **Cassidy**: flags pretty
> **Cassidy**: you're pretty

Not Cameron: you too gorgeous 😊
Not Cameron: I've always liked the term genderqueer.

> **Cassidy**: Talk in person about this, but thanks, you know, for being on the other end of the phone.

Not Cameron: Will always be, whenever you need me to be.

Eight

"I enjoy this, too much," Stephen said as he sat on the chair next to me, getting beautified.

I smirked as we both watched him getting his nails manicured. "Don't worry, I won't tell the football team," I said.

He laughed, shaking his head at me. "They already know. I sent them a snap. They're all insanely jealous."

"I love our football team," I said in a sigh, and he grinned at me.

"I fear that post-game we'll be in a salon now."

"I'll be joining you, if that is the case," I told him, before watching as my beautifier also manicured my nails.

"This seems excessive," Kennedy said as he came into our bathroom through his bedroom. "It's never usually this...."

"Intimate," I suggested. He hummed as Stephen lifted his hands towards Kennedy, grinning as he stroked over his cheeks.

"I like your cutthroat shaves though," Stephen told him before kissing him. "They make the events worth it."

"That isn't true," I said as I watched my nails get painted with a clear polish. Even the beautician had been upset to take off my lilac polish. We both agreed to be sad about it in equal measure as she shaped my nails.

"Is anything notable going on?" I asked.

Stephen shook his head dramatically at me. "I wouldn't know."

"It's not like you're the prime minister's son or anything," Kennedy said as he sat on the sink, and Stephen laughed.

"Maybe you should tell her that," he said, and Kennedy grinned.

Our school was full of notable sons. Sons of entrepreneurs, of theatre directors. Of chefs and lecturers, scientists, lawyers, and therapists.

We were the sons of a Member of Parliament, a prolific one at that, the brothers of one too, but Stephen was the son of our current prime minister.

Our current prime minister who was great for our country as a whole; she came in like a big warm hug after everything happened, fixing the mess of the country, raising the wage and generally feeling like everyone's really cool aunt.

I'd never had any issues with our prime minister Amelia Sinclair, until I found out her children were in fact not grown up, and that one of them was seventeen-year-old Stephen who she'd shipped off to boarding school so she didn't have to deal with his transition.

A seventeen-year-old Stephen who, when he walked with a protest against her decision to not change the law so that trans people could change their gender marker, she let him spend the night in a cell.

A seventeen-year-old Stephen who she hadn't seen since she took residence in Number Ten.

"Her term will be coming to an end," Stephen said idly as he examined his nails. "There *is* an election coming up."

"Do you think she's going to win?"

He shrugged. "It totally depends who's running against her."

"Very diplomatic of you," Kennedy told him; Stephen smiled.

"I listened in some of my etiquette classes," he told us. "I can also balance a book on my head, sip tea and masticate for the best of them."

"I can vouch for that," Kennedy said. I threw a cotton bud at him.

"You went to Princess School?" I said, and Stephen laughed.

"Course. How to sit and not spill, and *don't* even think about leaning over someone for the salt."

"I wish I'd gone to Princess School," I said in a sigh.

"No need, Queen," Kennedy said. I grinned at him as the bathroom door opened.

"Why aren't you dressed yet?" Harrison said, looking up from his phone to us. "*Why* are you just sitting here?"

"Nail care is important, Harrison," I told him as I

looked over him. He wasn't in his normal suit; this one was definitely new, a charcoal colour, slim fit and complemented by a charcoal waistcoat and blue tie.

"I swear, Cassidy."

"New suit?" I asked sweetly.

He sighed. "Special occasion," he told us, then, "Get *dressed*."

"Okay, okay," I said, standing, holding my hands up as I left our bathroom into my bedroom, unzipping my suit bag.

My spring suit was a heather grey, my bowtie a soft pink that I had to negotiate to hell and back to be allowed to wear. Kennedy's was a light blue, his tie a dark blue. Stephen's suit was that dark blue, his tie as light as Kennedy's suit. It was cute that they matched.

I told them as much as we were loaded into a town car, Harrison furiously tapping away at his phone.

"What's going on?" I asked him.

He sighed. "Nothing."

"You're a bad liar."

"I know," he muttered. I smiled as Kennedy shook his head.

"Are you getting sick again?" he asked softly. Harrison shook his head.

"No." He bit back then he looked up at us. "What? No. I'm not getting sick. I'm fine, honestly. I might have a stress headache, but I'm fine."

"So, what's going on?"

"Work stuff," he murmured. "Elections drawing near. It's the busiest my job will ever be."

"That's fair…" I said to Kennedy, who sighed. "What's Dom doing with your children?" I asked. Harrison looked at me, his expression softening instantly.

"Slumber party," he said, then he laughed. "In the garden, Wes and Millie have been set up in a tent, which I had to escape from when they dragged me into it in my suit." He smiled playfully. "Dom, however, is supplying regular food and snuggling up on the couch with Ryder who has already had a bath and is now sporting…" He dragged his thumb across his phone screen before turning it to me.

"Oh my gorgeous boy," I said in a coo as I took his phone, looking at the picture of Ryder sat on the couch, his fingers in his mouth, his pyjamas making him look like Tigger.

"How did you do that?" Stephen whispered. I looked at him. "He was Mr Stress Head, like the tension in this car was astronomical and then you just…"

"It's a superpower that comes with charisma," Kennedy muttered. I laughed as I swiped on the picture; the next was Ryder wrapped up in a towel that had little bear ears.

"Easy," I told Stephen. "Distract them with something they're passionate about. Usually gets them to calm down or distracts them enough that they forget they were stressed."

His phone buzzed in my hand.

"Father," I told him. I sighed as he took his phone back, frowning at it. His expression did a series of movements, none of them really committing to an emotion, and then the car stopped and we were ushered out into a small holding room.

My mum appeared in the room first.

"Yes," I told her, "yes, yes all the yes, you look stunning. *Who* is this?" I asked, taking my mum's hand, raising it above us. Her other hand rose, her clutch bag resting against the back of her head, a laugh playing on her lips.

"Rachel Gilbert," she told me.

I gasped. "I am here for it. It's the second-best outfit I've seen in the last hour," I told her. She frowned, shaking our hands together. "Well, Ryder dressed as Tigger kind of wins."

"Where is this picture of my grandson?" she asked. We both looked at Harrison who was glued to his phone again.

"He's stressed," I told her.

"Yes. As is…"

We looked towards the door together as Father came through it, his assistant Benjamin whispering feverishly to him.

"He," she said.

"What's going on?" I asked. She tapped her beautifully painted nails against her lip. "No one tells me anything." She tapped my shoulder then beckoned Kennedy to us, fixing his tie and brushing imaginary lint off his shoulders. She did the same to Stephen.

My mum was beautiful; I think she had in fact got somehow more beautiful as she'd got older. She had ginger hair like Kennedy and me, or I suppose, we had ginger hair like her. Hers was greying but it was almost unnoticeable. Luckily, Kennedy and I got most of our physical attributes from her. We hardly resembled our father as we were both slight and tall, our faces soft. No hard lines or cheekbones to *die* for.

"Rules," Father said. I turned to look at him as Kennedy practically stood to attention. "Neither of you will talk to any press tonight. At all, under any circumstance."

"Not even for a…" I began.

He cut me off pretty quickly. "You will act…"

"Straight?" Kennedy aided; Father rolled his eyes.

"Respectable," he snapped. "You will schmooze and charm, and not put a *fucking* toe out of place. You will not talk to press, or shag a member of staff."

"Crude," I said. Mum hit my shoulder so I bit my lip.

"Any step out of line, you will be removed and I have no qualms about doing it," he warned.

"Ah, now it feels like home," Stephen said. I grinned at him, and he winked back.

It was a stuffy event full of stuffy men in expensive suits. There was an orchestra, a full orchestra that I sat nearby with a flute of champagne watching as they – *the trumpet player* – played with ease.

"Who's this guy?" Stephen asked as he sat behind me.

I jumped then laughed. "What do you mean? There's no guy."

"You're not trying to hook up with *any*one," he said.

I laughed as I finished my champagne. "There is no

one shaggable here," I told him then turned on the seat, sitting sideways and leaning my arm on the back. He smiled at me.

"True," he said, nodding. "I mean, there's not even someone I'd say at a push." We both laughed as his eyes lingered around the room until they settled on Kennedy. "Although, he may turn my head," he added, clicking his tongue as Kennedy schmoozed alongside Mum who was laughing with her head thrown back.

"Don't know…" I said. "I feel like he's got a more attractive brother."

"Isn't he married?" he said, turning to look at me. I hissed at him. He grinned, his nose crinkling as he did.

I liked Stephen. I *really* liked Stephen and, considering I once would've been happy to never see him again, I marvelled at this. He was smart and quick, witty, brassy and attractive. He for all intents and purposes had balls and *that* was both the reason I hated him once, and like him now.

"You're…" I began. He frowned at me curiously so I sighed. "You're trans…"

"Wait, so that's why I don't have a dick?" he said, and I laughed.

"Stephen," I said.

"Yeah, I'm trans, why?"

"Well…" I began, then turned as Father took over the microphone.

"Thank you all for joining us at our event tonight," he started. I frowned at Stephen as I turned in my chair, looking at Father stood on the stage, Benjamin to his right, Mum to his left. "We've had an excellent time tonight so far, but now I think it's time to kick this celebration off."

There was a whisper across the room.

"Celebration, yes, because tonight, I have an announcement to make."

"He's pausing for effect," I told Stephen. He laughed softly as Kennedy sat behind him, squeezing his shoulder as he took the seat.

"Tonight, I would like to announce to you all, my friends, my family, my colleagues, that I am taking the job of leader of my party…" He paused. I turned to Kennedy with a whip. This time his pause had the desired dramatic effect. "Which, as I'm sure you've all figured out, means that in the next election you will be voting for *me* to be our next prime minister."

"What?" I said.

"*What?*" Stephen laughed.

"Oh my God," Kennedy moaned.

I sat on the kitchen counter next to the fridge, the tub of ice cream in my hand wrapped up in a tea towel so I could keep hold of it whilst eating it with a spoon.

The party had run late, so late that we came home rather than going back to the boarding house. We'd been swept up in men in expensive suits congratulating us on our father's success, telling us how much he deserved this opportunity, photo opportunities and raising glasses of champagne.

I wasn't nearly drunk enough for the amount of

champagne I'd drunk.

"Hey."

I sighed. "You can't sleep either?" I said, putting the spoon into my mouth and looking up as Stephen walked into the kitchen. He wobbled his head at me as if he wasn't all too sure what the correct answer was.

"Why, can't you?"

I shrugged, and he laughed.

"Where are the spoons?"

I pointed behind him, watching as he turned and got a spoon out of the drawer. He approached me warily, his eyebrow quirking at me as he stopped in front of me and took a spoonful of the ice cream.

"Unexpected announcement then…"

"It appears my father's running against your mum," I said.

"Yes. I don't even know which of the two of them I'd vote for… if I was old enough to."

"I'm voting for neither," I told him, and he smirked at me.

"You're not up thinking about that, though? Right?"

"Don't know, living in Number Ten," I said.

"It's not all it's cracked up to be," he said softly. "Granted, it was a lot of fun for the few months I was there when I was thirteen."

"Aren't you there in the summer?"

"No. I spend summers with my dad in the house I grew up in. She wouldn't like me to be seen."

"That's shitty of her," I said, nodding.

"Why did you ask me about being trans…" he asked,

then. "What did you start to ask me?"

I sighed, taking a bigger spoonful of ice cream. "When did you know?"

"That I was trans, or that I was a boy?"

"Are they two different answers?"

"Definitely," he said. I waved my hand at him. "I've known I was a boy since I was old enough to know the difference. So, three or four maybe? I've known that 'girl' didn't fit and it was wrong. I knew I didn't like being called 'she' and 'her'. I basically ignored everyone and anyone if they called me 'she', or my birthname, because I just didn't associate with them when I was younger."

"And trans?"

"I learnt the word trans when I was eleven. I was reading a book and one of the characters was trans, so I googled it, got in pretty deep."

"Naturally," I said, and he smiled.

"I figured that word described me, and I started telling anyone who'd listen that I'd found this word, this word trans and it literally describes me. What word have you found?" He whispered the question, almost so softly that I could've pretended that I'd missed it. He didn't push at it; he dug his spoon back into the ice cream, eating it from the spoon slowly.

"I don't know…" I said, but he didn't believe me. I sighed. "Genderqueer."

"Oh," he said, "interesting. What does genderqueer mean?"

"You don't know?" I said, and he laughed.

"I'm trans, not an encyclopaedia."

"It's like nonbinary," I told him, and he nodded once, telling me he obviously knew what that meant, "but I guess queerer." I smiled at him, and he laughed.

"Accurate."

"It just means there's no conforming to gender. Neither male nor female. Just..."

"Cassidy," he suggested.

"Just Cassidy." I nodded.

"That *does* make sense," he said.

I laughed as I ate more ice cream. "How come?"

"Well, you've never been conforming, have you? I mean, *ever*."

"I've just been me," I replied softly, looking away from him. He knocked my knee.

"And all things considered, that's the only way to be." He sighed. "Without sounding like a TV show presenter, have you always been looking for the word?"

"No," I said. "No, it didn't really occur to me that there *was* a word for me that wasn't just feminine or, I guess, camp."

"So, what made you look?"

"I lied," I told him. He frowned, shaking his head at me. "There is a guy."

"Oh," he said, amused.

"He's nonbinary. We got talking."

"I can tell you one thing for sure..." he said. I nodded softly. "Knowing *your* word and who you are is the best feeling."

"Even though your mum has never accepted you?"

"She is an obstacle, yes. It hurts, I'll never pretend it

doesn't. Sure, I put on a brave face. I have to; if she or anyone knew it was hurting me, they'd treat me differently."

"They wouldn't."

"Really? You don't think every time she came up on the screen or the news or whatever, Kennedy wouldn't ask me if it was okay?"

"Fair," I said softly. "Father wouldn't be happy with this development; he barely tolerates us being gay."

"Do you need his approval?"

"No," I said.

He smiled at me as he put his spoon into the sink. "Exactly," he said softly, then, "Tell me about this boy."

"I've *never* gossiped with you."

"Well, let's make it a thing."

Nine

A family meeting was called. A family meeting that involved Dom, all the grandkids, and Stephen. Kennedy and I had fought with Wesley for the *best* seat on the couch, whilst Mum sat happily cuddled up with Ryder on her knee. Harrison sat on the couch next to her, in sweats – like the rest of us, because it was Sunday and important things weren't supposed to happen on Sundays.

Stephen and Dom had laughed a lot and mocked us when they discovered even our sweats were branded. Ralph Lauren and Hugo Boss, even Calvin Klein – I'd reminded them that lounging was no excuse not to be stylish. I'd had nearly every pillow thrown at me.

We stopped fighting for the seat when Father walked into the room. We stopped instantly, not wanting to be shouted at as it definitely wasn't worth the headache. Kennedy won the seat; Wesley happily sat on his knee, his socked feet on my thighs.

"Okay…" Father said – he was *not* in sweats; he might as well have been in a suit. "Obviously you are all aware of my announcement last night," he continued, looking at each of us in turn as if daring us to disagree. Even Millie and Wesley didn't speak a word. I was impressed they already knew Grandfather wasn't worth the hassle.

I was even more impressed they didn't *once* act bored when Father began reeling off a list of rules that we *could not* break during his campaign.

"And finally," he added, his eyes drifting to Kennedy, who frowned up at him, "as I will be running against Amelia, I cannot allow this relationship to…"

We all cut him off by shouting at him at the same time. All of us except Stephen – even Ryder joined in by just making a noise.

"There's *no way*," Kennedy said, shaking his head as Harrison shouted.

"You're having a laugh; you can't be serious."

"John, you're being unreasonable," Mum said. He sighed and we all quietened.

"Sir…" Stephen said. We all looked at him. "With all due respect…" He looked back at us, his expression worried, but he soon shook it off. "Sir, I do not have a relationship with my mother. I haven't for a very long time. She doesn't even know I'm dating your son. It won't affect either of your campaigns, I can promise that, and I can also promise you that I love Kennedy and I will not be breaking up with him for any reason."

"Oh," Kennedy and I said together.

"You should marry him," Wesley told Kennedy. I laughed as Wesley grinned and Ryder wailed at us all.

"I'm not comfortable with having someone so close to us from the opposing…" Father began.

"John," Mum said in a sigh.

"I'm not voting for my mother," Stephen told him.

"Fine," Father snapped. "Just no acting…"

"Gay in public?" I suggested.

Father looked stressed. "You know you're on thin ice," he told me. "No spending my money, *no* flaunting your relationship…" He pointed at Harrison.

"Favourite child alert," I muttered; Kennedy laughed as Harrison smirked at us.

"You keep doing what you're doing."

I looked at Kennedy as he rolled his eyes.

"And all of you, *every* single one of you in this room. *No* talking to any reporters, or answering *any* questions. Got it?"

We remained quiet.

"Got it?"

"What should we do?" Wesley whispered. "He just told us not to answer any questions."

We walked side by side, laughing as we swapped our bubble teas. His was a milk tea as opposed to my fruit tea and I'd declared his an abomination the moment my card had been put into the pin machine. He'd protested loudly and it'd taken us three streets before I'd given in and agreed to swap our drinks.

He reached for my arm, turning me towards him, knocking the lid of my cup in his hand against his cup in my hand. He nodded softly then took a sip out of it, raising his eyebrow at me as if daring me to try it.

"I'm going to be devastated if I like this, you know," I told him as I stirred it with the straw. "I've played a big game, talked a big talk – if I like this…"

"Nothing you ever say again will be worth listening to?" he said. I gasped, pushing him by the shoulder, then finally drank through the straw.

It was one of the nicest things I'd ever drunk, so I schooled my face, my acting skills coming into play as I looked up at him.

"I was right."

He gasped, pushing me back again. "You *liar*. Oh my god, you *big* liar. Despicable." He shook his head and started running ahead of me, climbing up onto the half wall and balancing from one leg to the other. He reached the end before he sat himself on the wall, grinning at me as he drank from his cup. I walked towards him, standing between his swinging legs. "Where to now, Liar?" he asked.

I hit his knee before leaning my cup on his thigh. "Where do you want to go?" I asked.

He shook his head. "Bubble tea was my choice. It's your turn."

"We could go shopping," I offered, turning so I could point. "Oxford Street isn't too far."

"Oxford Street?" he repeated, then laughed. "Excuse me, I'm more Primark than Prada," he stated.

"*Excuse* me, Primark is on Oxford Street," I told him, and he almost barked out a laugh.

"The Queen has been to Primark?" he said.

I rose an eyebrow at him. "Course," I replied. "In disguise."

He laughed, shaking his head. "As much as I'd love to see that, I have about thirty pounds to my name to last me two weeks. I can't risk walking into a clothes shop right now."

"I could pay."

"You could *not*," he said pointedly. I frowned at him. "Sorry rich kid, but nuh-huh."

"I…" I began, then I shook my head. "I didn't mean…"

"I know," he said softly, resting his hand on my chest. "I know, don't worry. You've never had to count money, huh?"

"No," I said slowly.

He smiled, his fingers stroking up my chest to my hair. "What's that *like*?" he asked.

I laughed. "Awesome, I'm not going to lie."

"I can *only* imagine," he said in a sigh. "But just that. I'm just going to imagine, okay? You're not paying for anything."

"But…"

"No," he stated. I sighed as I looked down between us. "Nope. I love that you want to spoil me, honestly, but you've got to respect that I don't want you to."

"I do," I said, nodding. "I do, it's just a habit I guess."

"No, you want to spoil me. Learn your lines, Queen."

"Can I spoil you *sometimes*?" I asked.

He smirked then nodded slowly. "My birthday."

"Deal," I said, and he laughed happily.

"You have to do better than Cam's ballet boyfriend you realise, there is a bar and his ballet boyfriend bought him a snow globe with *Broadway* inside it for Christmas."

"Game on," I whispered, grinning up at him as he smiled around his straw.

"For now though…" he said slowly as he looked around where we were stood. "McDonalds."

"*What?*"

"Come on, Queen, let's get some chicken nuggets."

"You seem thoughtful," Finn whispered to me as he stroked my hair behind my ear from where he was lying next to me, on the floor of his office.

We'd pulled all the cushions from his little couch that he used for 'personal' meetings and scattered them around the floor for added comfort – as we'd found out quite quickly that his carpet was scratchy and unpleasant.

I guess no one planned for whichever teacher took residence in this office to be having sex on the floor – it was an oversight in my opinion.

"Cassidy," he said softly, so I looked up at him, then I sighed.

"I actually wanted to ask you something," I said as I stroked my fingers over the beaded cushion I was lying against.

Finn smiled at me. "You want to ask me something

as your teacher, or?"

"Or," I repeated. He hummed at me so I sighed. "This isn't going to sound like me at all, okay, and I know I couldn't say this to Kennedy, or even Theo."

"What, Cassidy?" he asked with a softness to his voice, so I closed my eyes.

"I've met a guy."

"You've met a guy?"

"Yeah, like a really amazing guy. I mean, I know I meet loads of guys. I know I fuck a lot of guys, but this guy. He's different. I feel it, and I want it to be, but I feel like…"

"You feel like you can't do it differently because you know this way too well."

"Yes," I whispered, then I sighed. "How stupid is that?"

"Not at all," he replied. I met his eyes. He smiled. "You're eighteen, Cassidy, and you do eighteen so well."

I frowned at him. He laughed.

"You have so much fun with your friends, you do what you want. You kiss who you want, you fuck who you want. You're so careful but so daring and I admire that so much. It's why you're the Queen, Cassidy, because you're doing the hardest years of your life so right." He paused. "This guy… who is he?"

"He's…" I sighed, then I laughed. "He's amazing."

"So you've said, give me a bit more."

"He plays the trumpet, and football, which I know, ew, but he kind of makes it hot. He loves musicals, and jazz. He wants to be a trumpet player in an orchestra pit one day, and he's so on that goal that I fully believe he'll do it. He's gorgeous inside and out. His personality is unflawed. Well, okay, fine, I guess he'll have a flaw somewhere, but nowhere it counts. It's so easy to fall for him."

"Is he in our orchestra?"

"No," I said slowly, and his eyebrow quirked. "He's a Golden Boy," I said. He gasped.

"Found his unforgivable flaw," he teased. I smiled as I buried my face into my hands. "Who is he? I know a lot of the Golden Boys."

"How?" I whispered.

He laughed. "Mel, the musical theatre teacher, is one of my friends. We talk a lot."

"He's on the music campus."

"So is her wife," he said. "Who is he?"

"Casper Murphy," I said quietly.

"Casper..." He mulled the name over then he laughed. "You're in love with a twin."

"Yes, but we'll pretend that isn't the important bit," I said.

"Are you looking for advice?"

"I guess."

"Well, advice. Go for it. Go for Casper. Be with him, enjoy him."

"As simple as that?"

"Yes," he said. "I presume that was the advice you gave to Kennedy about Stephen. They love each other, it's mad that it can be seen, but they do love each other. They don't care about anyone else, only each other and that's important. If I were you, I'd go on a date with him. A date that isn't going to end with sex, at least not straight away. I'd talk and be with him, not focusing on the physical parts of a relationship. Build up with him, work up to sex with him and it'll feel much better. So much more."

"You're the best sex I've ever had," I said, because it was true, and I wasn't one to not pay a compliment. Finn laughed but he smiled as if he was made up.

"Thank you, Queen," he said. "But now you should start a new adventure."

"The adventure of being in a relationship?" I asked, and he nodded slowly. I winced. "Does this mean we have to stop doing *this*?"

"Afraid so," he answered.

I groaned, falling back onto the cushions we were lying on. "Can we pretend I didn't say anything and do it one more time?"

He looked at me, so I grinned then gasped as he climbed on top of me, pinning my arms by my head and kissing me deeply.

Ten

*Remember that date I told you about...
Saturday, 7.30pm. I hear there's a new musical in
town. Dress up to the nines. I expect black tie, you
look best in it xoxo*

Theo smirked at me in the mirror as I turned from left to right, checking out the suit jacket I was wearing. It was royal blue, a floral pattern, but tasteful, of course. It was gorgeous, classy, but *somewhat* flamboyant.

"What?" I asked Theo.

He laughed. "Why are we buying a new suit?"

"Jacket," I corrected him.

"Jacket," he repeated. I laughed, turning fully to him. He grinned at me, nodding to tell me he thought I should buy it.

"I might have a date," I said softly, "an important one that requires fancy clothes."

He smiled. It looked genuinely happy. "Can I ask details?"

I wobbled my head at him. "I don't want to commit to answers just yet. Sunday, after it."

"Okay…" he paused. "You should buy it."

"Not too much?"

"For Queen Cassidy, certainly not."

"How much is it?" I asked the assistant. She smiled pleasantly at me, straightening out my shoulders, fixing the lapel.

"Just a mere two thousand," she said, then stared me down in the mirror as if trying to make me believe I couldn't afford it, which would ultimately make me want it more.

I could afford it. I definitely had the money in my savings, but I didn't want to spend it. Not on a jacket, at least.

I met her eyes in the mirror. They were challenging me.

"I'll take it," I said. She smiled, nodding to me, then walked away from me. "*Fuck*," I added.

Theo laughed from behind me. "Cassidy," he said in a gasp as he came to stand next to me.

"She was giving me *that* look. She thought I couldn't afford it."

"You can't…"

"I can," I said in a laugh. "I can."

He rose his eyebrow at me then sighed. "This is gorgeous. I don't regret it even though it's your jacket."

"Theo," I moaned.

He laughed, knocking his head against mine. "I'll work the street corners with you to pay it off."

"I love you," I told him, kissing him lightly, so he laughed.

"How will you be paying for this?" the assistant asked. I looked at Theo's reflection then turned to the lady.

"Through an account," I confirmed. She nodded at me before taking the jacket off for me and putting it into a suit bag. We walked together to the cashier.

"What's the account name?" she asked, her perfectly manicured nails hovering above the keyboard. I sighed.

"John Bradford," I answered. She nodded, typing onto the keyboard, her smile shifting to her customer service smile that was only received when they felt you could *actually* afford what you were buying.

"Thank you, Mr Bradford, that has gone through."

Shit.

Father is Calling...

I slid my phone back into my pocket, shaking my head and straightening out my jacket, checking my face in the mirror. I looked *nervous*.

No.

Come on.

Come on, Cassidy. There was no need to be nervous. I was almost completely sure I was going on a date with Casper, as it *definitely* wasn't Finn, and Casper hadn't returned a message to me for the entire day.

This was going to be perfect.

I just needed to look less wide-eyed.

Father is Calling...

"Go away," I whispered, shaking my head at my phone. "I'll deal with you tomorrow." I shook out my arms, took a few deep breaths in, reapplied my eyeliner and finally left the bathroom.

There was already quite a crowd forming outside the theatre. The gorgeously lush red carpet stretched far outside, people walking it and talking animatedly to other people with outstretched recorders.

I recognised Noah, the boy who ran the theatre school blog. He'd left Goldstein a handful of years ago and *always* turned up at these events. He wore a nice-looking suit. I told him as much.

"Cassidy Bradford," he said in a laugh as his eyes examined me. "I've heard a few rumours that you have been rendezvousing with Golden boys."

"I neither confirm nor deny these rumours," I said, and he laughed.

"Is the Queen looking for a King Consort?"

"Always," I answered softly.

"Are you coming to the show tonight?" he asked, grinning. I nodded. "Waiting for someone?"

"Maybe," I said, looking back at him over my shoulder. He smirked at me, lifting his pen to his mouth and chewing on it. I sighed.

"If they don't turn up, you can come home with me."

"Promises, promises," I purred as I watched a car

pull up. A beautiful man got out of the car, smiling a movie star smile as he rebuttoned his jacket. He greeted the carpet as if this kind of thing was a regular occurrence for him. The car door closed behind him, but bounced back open pretty quickly.

"Devon," I said as he, too, fixed his jacket then his hair, looking almost as nervous as I felt. His eyes scanned the carpet before they landed on me.

He appeared shocked to see me before looking away from me, so I went to him.

"What are *you* doing here?" I said sharply.

He looked back at me, his expression hardening instantly. "My Dad owns the theatre…" he spat back at me. "Do your research. What are *you* doing here?"

"None of your business," I muttered as I looked around again.

"Waiting for someone?" he asked.

"None of your business," I repeated. "Who's that?" I asked as the beautiful man continued ahead. Devon scowled after him. "Mortal enemy?" I asked.

Devon scoffed. "My brother."

"So, yes," I said, nodding.

He laughed, covering his mouth when I looked at him. "I thought you liked your brothers."

"Most days," I said, and he shook his head, amused.

"*He's* already working with Dad – going to take over the theatres when Dad retires. I don't think he has peripheral vision."

"I didn't know you had a brother."

"Funny," he said. "Usually people don't know *he* has

a brother."

We looked at each other for the first time since we'd started this conversation.

"Devon, come on," the beautiful man said. Devon scowled at him.

"I have a spare ticket, if you…"

"They'll be here," I said. He shrugged as I lifted my wrist to read my watch. "I'm sure of it."

"Okay," he said softly, walking away down the carpet. I decided *not* to watch him go; instead, I got my phone out of my pocket.

Missed Calls: Father (3)

Nothing else.

I rubbed my forehead, dropping my phone back into my pocket and patting down my jacket until I found a cigarette. I walked around the crowd, leaning against the stage door as I lit the cigarette and raised it to my lips. I held it there as I got my phone out.

I went to text Casper, but decided I wasn't going to beg. *If* he wasn't going to turn up, I didn't want to let him know that I'd even noticed his lack of presence.

Instead, I called Father back.

"It's about *damn* time you picked up your phone," he growled at me. I sighed, leaning my head back and blowing the smoke upwards as he ranted at me, not pausing long enough for me to even think about replying. "So that's it, Cassidy, you're cut off, you hear me? I will *not* be paying into your account anymore; you will *not* have access to any of my accounts. You are cut off."

"Talk about family values. I hope that isn't one of

your promises," I murmured.

"Cut *off*, Cassidy," he stated. "No negotiation."

He hung up on me.

"*Fuck*," I whispered, then turned as the bell rang in the theatre. I threw my cigarette, stepping on it before rounding the building. I stopped when I saw Devon stood in the doorway. He looked towards me, smiling at me as he held up his tickets.

"I was wondering where you'd gone," he said as I walked up the steps towards him.

"Why are you giving me your ticket?"

"It'd be a travesty for that suit jacket not to get the exposure it deserves."

"True," I said softly, taking the ticket from him and following him into the theatre. The orchestra was playing the overture as I followed Devon up to his seats.

"Quite the view," I said softly as he lifted the complimentary programme from the seat and gestured his hand towards me.

"Great for throwing peanuts at peasants," he whispered back. I laughed, covering my mouth with the programme as the lights dimmed and the curtain rose.

"Who didn't turn up for the Queen?" Devon asked after we'd been given our interval snacks. I shook my head at him, continuing to read through the programme.

"I didn't know you liked musicals," I questioned, and he laughed.

"You're deflecting," he said. "I've always loved theatre. When I was small, I used to come with Dad when he sat in rehearsals. I'd sit by him for all of five minutes, usually just the opening number, *then* I'd be on that stage and they'd humour me. Sure, it was probably because I was the boss's son, but they'd teach me the choreography, let me sing with them."

"Why did you join the choir then?" I asked.

"I didn't think I'd make it in the theatre," he sighed, wincing as he did. I rose my eyebrow at him. "I can sing, sure. I'm not going to act all coy, I *can* sing, but I'm nowhere as good as the boys in the theatre. Nowhere as good as you."

"We could've been friends," I said.

"*Really?*" he laughed.

"If you'd have auditioned for the theatre, yeah, but you didn't and then you were a dick to Kennedy, so…"

"I know," he said shaking his head. "I know it was stupid. I've been reminded about that every day since I broke up with Kennedy."

"You took his virginity spitefully," I said. "That's a dick move."

"I know," he said. "I know and I regret it. Honestly. I've lost friends, I've totally fallen from grace. I won't even show my face in the theatre or when the orchestra are performing. I regret it every day."

"So, did you give me the ticket to beg for forgiveness?"

"No," he answered softly, "because it's not you who I need forgiveness from, it's Kennedy. I gave you the ticket because you were stood up."

"I *wasn't.*"

121

"Cassidy. I've made some stupid decisions but I'm not an idiot."

I sighed, shaking my head at him. "Thank you," I said. "Don't you dare tell anyone someone stood up the Queen. I have a reputation to uphold."

"And I have a habit of destroying those," he said. I smiled. He grinned straight back.

"Master Walker…"

We both turned as a very well-dressed steward stood behind us with a tray against his stomach.

"Would you like a drink?"

"Yes, please," Devon answered, then looked at me, raising an eyebrow. "Champagne?"

"What are we celebrating?" I asked, amused.

He shrugged. "Nothing. That's why we should have champagne."

"Well, cheers"

I walked with Devon back to the boarding house. We walked with our hands in our pockets, a definite space between us, but we were together. *That* was undeniable.

We were together, and there were a few champagnes soaking into my insides and sex was on the cards. Which, admittedly, was a surprise even to me but it was there; sex was totally an option.

He turned to look back at me, smiling as he swiped his card to let us into the boarding house. We walked the sapphire corridor quietly.

I'd walked it before; well, I'd walked most of the corridors before. Boy after boy, night after night, jumping from room to room. I'd never been in Devon's room, though. I'd never slept with *any* of the boys from the choir, especially not his gaggle of bitches.

"Where will your… friends be?" I asked.

He laughed as he continued ahead of me. "Out. It's Saturday," he said with a shrug. "Theatre visits and gala dinners and whatnot," he added, then, "Why?"

"No reason," I replied.

"Yeah sure," he said softly as he unlocked his bedroom door. His room was immaculate. Even *my* room wasn't immaculate but there wasn't a thing out of place. He looked at me over his shoulder, taking his suit jacket off and hanging it over his bed knob. He turned to look at me as he undid his shirt cuffs.

"I'm just using the restroom, make yourself comfortable," he offered. I nodded to him as he smiled, pushing his sleeves to his elbows, then going into his bathroom. I sat on the end of his bed, reaching into my pocket for my phone.

My father hadn't tried to contact me again, but Kennedy had. I decided to ignore his message, figuring I could look at that later. I paused when I saw *Not Cameron*.

I clicked on his message.

Not Cameron: So, how are you spending tonight?
Not Cameron: If you're not busy you could come see me.

    Cassidy: That was my plan after all.

Not Cameron: What??

> **Cassidy**: Pretty sure we were supposed to be on a date tonight.

Not Cameron: Not in my diary

> **Cassidy**: Sure

Not Cameron is calling...

> *Decline*

Not Cameron is calling...

> *Decline*

Not Cameron: Answer your DAMN phone!
Not Cameron is calling...

"I answered, happy?"

"What are you talking about, Cassidy? We never arranged a date or anything."

"You sent me notes…"

"Come again?" he said. I shook my head then lifted my phone from my ear, sending him a video request. He answered pretty quickly but he was frowning.

"I needed to see your face," I said. He shook his head. "I need to know you're telling me the truth when I ask you this question… Did you send me notes?"

"No," he said quickly, then, "Why would I, Cassidy? We've been meeting up, and if we're not together we text. Why'd I send you notes; *how* would I send you notes?"

"I…" I shook my head. "I don't know; they were in my locker. I just assumed that… that it was you, because it wasn't Finn…" I said. He shook his head.

"No, Cassidy."

"So you didn't stand me up tonight."

"Excuse me, you think I'd have the audacity to stand the Queen up? No way, uh-huh. I *like* you, Cassidy. I was performing tonight; I had a gig which I was *going* to invite you to but obviously that's ended."

"You need to tell me how that went. I have something to deal with right now, but tomorrow maybe, I want to hear how it went."

"Okay," he said softly. I nodded, looking towards the bathroom as the door clicked open. "We're okay, Cassidy," he said. I looked back at the screen. "Me and you. We're okay, and we'll talk about the thing neither of us are saying. Okay?"

"Okay," I said softly then blew him a kiss. He winked at me before hanging up. I stood, putting my phone into my pocket, then turned to Devon.

He stopped looking back at me, frowning at me as he examined me.

"What?" he said.

"I have a question," I said. "How did you know I'd been stood up?"

"Oh," he shrugged. "I guessed." I rose an eyebrow at

him. "What?"

"How did you *know* I didn't have the tickets, that I wasn't supposed to be there. How did you know?"

"I didn't know…" he said.

"Devon."

He rolled his eyes. "Fine." He shrugged. "I thought I'd at least get a shag before you figured it out."

"Sex was *not* on the table," I lied.

"Oh yeah, and you don't love musicals," he said.

I rolled my eyes. "Why the *fuck* would you want to sleep with me?"

"The King *and* the Queen, in one year. I'd be revered."

"Oh, sweetheart, you're delusional," I told him, then walked towards him. "Now tell me what the *fuck* is going on."

He looked away from me.

"I swear to God, Devon," I growled at him; he narrowed his eyes at me.

"Who were you talking to?" he said. I shook my head at him. "Because it wasn't Finn."

"Finn," I repeated. "What are you talking about?" I asked.

"I get it, I get it… our little secret, xoxo," he whispered. I pushed him back. He hit the wall behind him.

"You sent the notes."

"Well done," he said, a sickly grin on his face. I balled my hands into fists, resisting the urge to punch the smugness off his face.

"How did you know about Finn?" I hissed.

"You *told* me," he relished in saying.

I shook my head at him. "Tell me the truth."

"I *am*," he shouted back at me.

"When the…" I said, then, "Valentine's."

"You got pretty drunk, Your Majesty. You got all up in my face and you told me that you'd never want to have sex with me, and you didn't need to anyway because you were fucking Finn."

"I was *drunk*."

"Yeah, yeah sure but then I saw you with him and yeah you guys are *not* subtle, so I figured I could prove you wrong, I could get you to fuck me, then…"

"I would never have."

"Do you lie to yourself often? You were practically a cat on heat coming in here."

"Then what?" I asked.

His eyes practically glittered. "I hear your father's running for prime minister," he said.

I shrugged. "And? What do you want, an autograph?"

"It'd be a shame if a scandal like his gay son fucking a teacher at a prestige boarding school got out."

I laughed harshly at him. "Oh, sweetheart, do your research. If he was on fire and I had water, I'd drink it. You might've been able to get to Kennedy through our father, but not me." I pushed him back again before turning to walk away from him.

"Your father, no…" he said. I stopped at the door. "But I'm pretty sure Finn would lose his job."

I gripped the door tightly.

"Fucking a student must be *quite* a punishable offence, wouldn't you say? And the future prime minister's son. I'm pretty sure he'd be struck off quicker than, well, quicker than I almost got you into bed."

"What do you get out of this?" I growled at him. "What the *fuck* is your goal here?"

"You embarrassed me," he spat at me. I turned to look at him. "You *and* Kennedy, you shamed me, destroyed me. You've seen how quickly the choir has fallen from grace because suddenly the King and the Queen decree it."

"You did this to yourself. You *used* Kennedy, you used me."

"You were stupid enough to believe a teacher would love you enough to ask you on a date."

"I didn't think the notes were from Finn, you *idiot*."

He appeared confused for all of a second.

"What do you want me to do?" I asked, shaking my head.

"Well, as you asked," he said softly, walking towards me. He stopped in front of me, reaching up to touch my face. I grabbed his wrist, squeezing it in my hand. He fisted his hand.

"I want the Choir to be on top. I want you to make us popular again. I can't be having the footballers in better standing than us."

I pushed him away from me. "No."

"Then I tell someone about Finn. Who first? Your father, or a reporter, or our headmaster?"

"You wouldn't dare," I growled.

"But you know how I like to send notes," he said, then he laughed. "They're so easy to write without anyone knowing it's you, you know. I'm sure Kennedy's scratching his head about the one I sent him," he continued. I frowned at him, reaching into my pocket and swiping open the unread message from Kennedy.

The King: We need to talk. Seriously.

"I told Kennedy all about Finn. I have no reservations about telling other people," he said, then shrugged at me. "A whisper in an ear is *all* it takes to start a rumour."

"No one would believe you," I said.

He smirked. "No, maybe not, but if an allegation is made, it *has* to be taken seriously. Finn will be fired anyway, and I guess that means no musical." He covered his mouth. "Oh dear."

Eleven

"You tell me what the fuck is going on, right now," Kennedy spat at me, and I saw red. I turned to look at him, and he must have seen something, as he took a step backwards.

"You do not talk to me like that," I said as I stepped towards him. He took another back. "You do not raise your voice, you do not swear at me, and you certainly do not order."

"Cassidy..."

I held my hand up, and he stopped.

"You want to know something, you ask, and I will tell you, Kennedy. I always will, but you do *not* order me around. You are not our father, Kennedy, and you do not want to become like him."

"I'm just confused."

"Then ask, don't demand," I said, softening my voice just a little, but not enough to let him put his guard down.

"Cassidy, I'm sorry," he said, his voice weak. I didn't let my posture relax. He looked hurt. "I'm confused, and I don't understand what has been going on. You tell me everything, Cassidy, everything, but you didn't tell me… this."

"You didn't need to know this," I replied, then sat on my bed, He sat on his own, his knees bumping mine.

"Cassidy," he said.

"Finn…" I leant my head back, letting out a sigh. "Finn…"

He had always been my allocated teacher. The teacher I should go to for advice, for academic reasons, personal reasons, any reason in fact. Every first year is given a teacher; Kennedy's and Cody's was Otis. Theo's and mine was Finn. We met practically weekly to talk through everything, until puberty, really. The moment my voice had fully broken when I was fourteen our meetings became monthly, and then they were supposed to become termly.

He, of course, was also our theatre teacher, and I'd been a staple in the theatre since I first stepped into our school and bonded with Finn almost instantly. He was a new teacher when I started, still in university doing his teacher training. He was only nineteen himself, but had already been pretty much guaranteed a job when he graduated. Which was why he was given some first years to look after.

He was gorgeous, I was aware of it even when I was just eleven, but I knew there was no way that was going to happen.

Until it did.

We started flirting when I was sixteen. It was pretty unintentional, at least on his part. I flirted with him and he responded; it'd have been impolite not to. When I was seventeen, we bumped into each other in one of the better gay bars near to the school. He had laughed, a laugh so full of joy, and told me I shouldn't be there.

I, having been served one too many alcoholic drinks, especially since I was just seventeen, had to practically promise myself to the bouncer to get him to let me in.

I had been prowled a lot, because I was a twink and I was more than willing to go home with someone. I'd been having sex with boys in school and, although none of them were experienced, at that point that was what I wanted.

Finn had found me before someone far more dangerous.

He'd stood next to me, leaning on the bar and insisted I go back to the boarding house. When I'd refused, he told me he wouldn't leave me alone until I left. I told him I wasn't leaving until I was guaranteed sex.

He'd mulled this over and I'd seen it. I saw him consider offering it to me; in the end, he decided not to and told me he'd walk me back. I was shocked, but more concerned, and I asked him why, and why he'd give up his own chance at sex to walk me home and make sure I wasn't out getting into trouble.

He simply laughed and told me he'd gone out for a drink, not for sex.

I told him he was a liar.

He told me I was stupid.

I told him he should just leave me.

He told me he'd never do that.

I asked him why.

He told me he cared about me.

I blushed and told him he looked very nice tonight.

He tutted and told me I shouldn't be flirting.

I reminded him we'd been flirting all year.

He laughed, swore we hadn't.

I called him a liar, and informed him he'd lied to me twice in ten minutes and that wasn't good as he was my teacher.

The word teacher seemed to affect him; it was almost as if it reminded him I was one of his *students*, not just a guy he'd met in a bar.

We'd walked quietly for a few minutes and I'd thought of more than enough things to say to break the silence, but by the time I felt they were formulated enough for me to say them, we were back at the school.

He stopped just before we went in.

He smiled at me, telling me I shouldn't sneak into gay bars, that I should wait until I'm eighteen and if he finds me there again, he'll have no qualms about turning me in.

I laughed, telling him he wouldn't.

He said, *try me*.

I told him that was hot.

He rolled his eyes, but the smile was unmistakeable.

I kissed him on the cheek, and said thank you for bringing me home.

He told me we couldn't do this.

I asked him what this was, because we weren't doing anything.

He kissed me.

He had put his hand on my chest and told me, *I can't feel this way about you. You're just a kid, and not even just a kid, you're one of my students and that's, that's so wrong.*

I kissed him again.

I'm eighteen in September, I had said. *We'll talk then.*

"It started when you were eighteen."

"Yes," I sighed, then I rubbed my forehead. "The Monday after our birthday."

"Fuck, Cassidy, what the hell, why didn't you tell me?"

"You were all wrapped up in Stephen and fucking Devon; my god, there was so much going on. Then you broke your elbow and, Kennedy, you had so much going on before Christmas that there was never the right time to sit you down and tell you I was... having sex with Finn."

"Having sex," he repeated. I looked at him. "Not just fucking him?"

"No," I whispered, then I winced. "It hurts. Devon actually found my weak spot. That bitch figured it out and tried to get to me by using Finn and it hurts so much, Kennedy. If it gets out it could completely jeopardise his job and I can't be the reason Finn loses his job."

"Are you still having sex?"

"No, we already agreed to stop, but that was for a completely different reason," I said. He frowned at me then shook his head, rubbing the bridge of his nose.

"What are you going to do?"

"Hit Devon with something heavy."

"Yeah, after that."

"I don't know. I need to talk to Finn. He'll probably know what to do."

"So, he sleeps with students a lot then?" he asked. I growled at him, He shrugged. "How else would he know what to do? He's not this great oracle just because he's twenty-seven. He's us with a job," he said. I laughed into my hands, shaking my head then running my fingers through my hair. "I take it that it isn't a relationship."

"No," I said quietly, "I was sleeping with other people. You know that. We weren't exclusive, but my god Kennedy, no one compared to him."

I took a deep breath then knocked on Finn's office door. He beckoned me in from inside. I opened the door then smiled when I saw him sat on the floor in front of his desk, in joggers and a t-shirt with the slogan *The Show Must Go On*, from when the world went into lockdown a few years back.

He took my breath away and he wasn't even doing anything.

"Why hello, Cassidy," he said. I sat opposite him, pulling at a strand in the rip of my jeans. He had our script laid out in front of him, next to his book, *the* bible of the entire musical. It had every stage direction, lighting cue, prop, and set piece inside it. It was Finn's pride and joy.

"What's today's job?" I asked.

He shook his head, amused. "Officially, nothing, but I'm a perfectionist and feel like I'll find *something* if I just keep looking through it."

"Oh," I said amused.

He smiled, closing the book's back over. "What's up, Cassidy?" he asked. "Has something happened with that boy…"

"No," I answered weakly, then, "no, things with Casper are pretty good, honestly. It's something else…"

"Okay," he said. I looked straight at him. "I've never known our Queen lost for words."

"Please don't get mad," I said.

He frowned at me. "Cassidy."

"Devon knows…"

"Devon *knows*?"

"About us."

"Shit," he said, then stood.

"Please don't be mad."

"I'm not mad," he said. I stood with him. He turned to look at me. "Devon, why *him*? Out of every boy you could've told, why Devon?"

"I didn't tell him," I snapped at him. He met my eyes.

"Don't snap at me," he said simply. I looked down. "Don't turn this into an argument, Cassidy, tell me what happened."

"He found out," I said. "He's threatening to tell. He's… he's…" I covered my mouth. He sighed, pulling me towards him and hugging me. I buried my face into his chest, trying to make sure he didn't know that I was crying.

I was sure he knew.

But he was doing the decent thing and not mentioning it.

"Cassidy," he said softly. "We can't see each other right now." I hugged him tighter. He sighed. "Not until we figure this out. We can't be seen together. It's too risky. I *love* you Cassidy and I need to protect you."

"No," I said weakly, "no, it's not me who's in trouble, it's you."

"I'll be okay, Cassidy," he said softly, "I will. We just, can't do this. We've got to be even more careful than we've ever been."

I sighed, taking a step away from him, wiping my face, threading my fingers through my hair.

"You're right," I said, nodding. "No, no you're right. I'm sorry." I went to leave. "Finn…" I said, turning back to him. He nodded as he bit his nail whilst leaning on his desk. "You're a teacher, is there any way you can expel him?" I asked. He smiled at me. I grinned back then blew a kiss to him. I left his office, took a deep breath then continued down the hallway out into the yard and began to run.

I weaved myself amongst the trees deep into the wooded area around the school, deeper and deeper until I tripped. I tumbled head-first over the log my foot had connected with then I crumbled to the floor.

Breathing in.

And back out.

In.

Then back out.

My hands covered my eyes, my knee throbbing where it'd connected with the floor.

"You're okay," was whispered into my ear, then I was sat up. "We can do this."

I was pulled into a body. One hand in my hair, the other wrapped around me.

"How did you find me?"

"You ran past me. I chased after you pretty quickly," Cody said. I looked at him. He smiled at me; it was soft as he threaded my hair through his fingers, pushing it back from my face. "Why are you on the floor?"

"I fell," I said meekly. He sighed. "Do you…"

"I know," he said then tilted his head. "Finn, huh?"

I looked at him.

"I am *impressed* but not surprised."

"That's my aim," I said. He laughed, knocking his elbow against mine. "This is a mess," I added in a sigh. "Devon, *fucking* Devon out of everybody, and he's blackmailing me, and *then* my father cuts me off. Just like that. No more money, nothing."

"What?" he said softly. I groaned. "Okay, okay. Let's *relax*." I nodded into my hands then looked at him through my fingers as he held a joint to me. "And I think I *need* to know some gossip about Finn."

I smirked at him as he shrugged.

"I want the gossip before the shit hits the fan."

"True friendship that, Cody," I said, softly lifting my

hips so I could get my lighter out of it.

"Oh, I'll try my best to help you to solve it. I've been shouting at Kennedy for the last hour or so because he's got no right to be so righteous about this. We didn't know your money had been cut off."

I nodded, groaning as I took the joint from him. I put it into my mouth and lit it.

"Ah," Harrison said as he opened his front door. I looked away from him.

"Kennedy suggested I talk to you," I offered meekly. "He figured you might be able to help me."

"With the money, no I don't think so," he said as he let me in. I walked into the living room, smiling at Ryder as he sat on the floor chewing on a teething ring. It was soon rejected when he saw me and crawled towards me.

"Hello," I said softly as I picked him up. He gasped happily, grabbing onto my collar.

"Cass… Cass."

I gasped at him, bouncing him on my arm.

"Are you saying Cassidy?" I asked. He grinned at me before laughing and headbutting my shoulder. I looked at Harrison as he smiled.

"He's getting there," he said softly before stroking Ryder's hair. "I'm more impressed he can tell the two of you apart, to be honest."

"He likes me better than Kennedy," I said, then turned when he touched my shoulder.

"What's happened, Cassidy?"

"Father told you about cutting me off?"

"Oh, he bitched about you all the way through Sunday lunch," he told me. I sighed as I sat on the floor, letting Ryder go again. "A two-thousand-pound jacket?"

"It looks good," I said, then shook my head. "But that isn't why I'm here."

"What have you done?" he asked.

"How assuming of you," I said. He rose an eyebrow at me. "I've been sleeping with my theatre teacher."

"Oh."

"Kennedy suggested I come talk to you because…"

"Because of Preston?" he asked. I lowered my eyes. "Be a bit more specific."

"Because it was an affair, and you had to keep it quiet and, I don't know, but I'm lost. I'm so lost and I just, I really, really like Finn. I don't want our relationship to end, at least not the friendship side of it, and right now I just feel like I've lost him." I looked up at Harrison, and then…

And then we're six. It was nearing summer, the summer holidays quickly approaching. Mum had picked us up from school and we were babbling either side of her, neither of us taking a breath because we had to tell our mum every single detail of our day. We're excited because we're six and we love our mum and we want her to be as happy as we are.

Then we get home, and Father is muttering to himself, throwing on his coat and swearing under his breath as he looks for things.

Something has happened. I need to go and pick up Harrison.

Something has happened.

And suddenly, Kennedy and I are not so excited, not babbling as much. We're quiet and we're scared but we don't know why. Father was never a warm man. He'd always been pretty cold. Emotionless, at least to me. We never shared a hug; we barely shared a smile. But I knew my father was a strong man. I knew because he spoke to other men in suits a lot and he stood up in that place Mum calls Parliament and shouts at men stupider than himself, and somehow gets them to listen. I knew he was strong, I knew he was brave, and right now I knew he was scared.

And that scared the living daylights out of me, because if my father was scared then something really bad had happened, and it had happened to Harrison.

He disappeared away to the big, beautiful school that Harrison went to. The school that one day Kennedy and I would go to.

The school we'd one day rule.

Harrison had told us all about the school, about the theatre, about the band. He'd told us everything he could think of whenever he came home for break. He'd told us about his friends, about Riley and Mason, and Preston. Oh, Preston, his very best friend in the entire world, and how he loved him, how he loved him with his whole heart. He had whispered to us, when we were three, of how Preston was his boyfriend and he was sure he would be forever.

He had told us with tears in his eyes when we were five that they'd broken up and he had felt broken.

141

And now, now we were six, and something had happened.

Harrison had come home with Father. He didn't say anything to anyone, just went upstairs to his bedroom.

I drew him a picture to make him feel better. It had a rainbow and a bright sunshine with a smiling face. I went to give it to him but Mum stopped me, taking me back to our playroom and telling Kennedy and me that something had happened, and Harrison was really very sad. He needed to be alone for a little while.

We both nodded like we understood, but we didn't really, and once Mum had left us alone, I snuck to Harrison's room and slipped the picture underneath his door, because I understood he needed to be alone, I just didn't understand why.

Kennedy and I still shared a room then. The other, which would become my room when we were ten, being our playroom. Mum had tucked us into bed that night, kissing our cheeks and blowing raspberries on our necks, making us giggle babyishly and happily. She turned out the light, leaving just our lamp on that projected stars around the room.

We didn't sleep, not right away; we never did. But we both faked sleep when the door opened. Harrison laughed. It wasn't a proper laugh by any means; it was sad and there was a pain there. At six I had no idea what that meant, but he laughed because his baby brothers were doing a ridiculous job at persuading him we'd gone to sleep. When we realised it was Harrison, we showed him we were awake, because obviously he didn't already know, then he climbed into my bed with me. He cuddled me close and when Kennedy jumped out of his bed and into mine, he cuddled him close too.

He thanked me for my picture in a quiet whisper and I cuddled him tighter, then Kennedy asked him why he was sad. Harrison had sighed but he told us that Preston had died, and he was very, very upset because he'd loved Preston a lot.

We cuddled him closer.

We were ten before he told us that Preston had killed himself. He told us before we started at Ravenwood, in case it was brought up and we were caught unaware, and as we grew older and older, he told us more and more about Preston. About their relationship, about their affair when they were eighteen, about how they'd planned to go to university together and start afresh in London. He told us how he still didn't understand what had led Preston to his decision. He'd read the note countless times, and still it made no sense.

He wore Preston's tree of life necklace every day.

"You haven't lost him," Harrison now said, with no annoyance in his voice, something I marvelled at because I would've gone off at any bitch who'd said that to me. "Not by any means." He paused. "But, he is your teacher and that's… problematic."

"Yeah, I know that," I muttered. He sighed, coming to sit beside me. Ryder found this to be the most exciting thing ever and pushed himself onto his feet, walking towards his daddy. He babbled away at him, punctuating it with 'dada' occasionally.

"Finn's an adult," he said. I met his eyes because I was ready to shout back at him, but I could tell he hadn't finished his sentence. He'd just paused to kiss Ryder's tiny hands. "He's not going to be as... dramatic, should we say, as if you were with another teenager. He'll be somewhat logical; he knows how dangerous this is. He knows his job's on the line and he'll be figuring out a way he can keep his job, without harming his relationship with you."

"We're not in a.... relationship," I muttered. Harrison rose his eyebrow at me. "It's my own fault," I continued. "I'd told him about Cas, and we agreed to stop doing our thing because we both thought it'd be a good idea to see what happens with Cas, but then Devon..."

"You're worried about?"

"Him losing his job," I said, shaking my head. "I still want to be his friend. I don't want him to hate me."

"He won't hate you," he said softly, then shook his head. Ryder giggled, shaking his head back. "I can guarantee that."

"Did Riley hate you?" I asked.

Harrison sighed. "No." He scrunched his nose at me. "I wished he had, I really did, but when he found out about our affair, he nodded and told me he expected it; he knew we still loved each other and he was surprised it hadn't happened sooner."

"What do I do then?"

"Back off," he offered. "Give Finn time to figure something out, and *don't* give Devon any ammo. Just go quiet. Go to rehearsal, go to class, nothing else."

"Is that what you did?" I asked.

He laughed in a cough. "When Preston and I were sleeping together?" he asked. I nodded slowly. "Kind of. We almost made too much of an effort to not touch each other in public or be alone together. We worked too hard – honestly. Which is what you shouldn't do," he sighed. "Who's Cas?"

"Ah yes, Cas. The other part in all this," I said. "*Casper* is the person I actually really like."

"Ah."

145

Twelve

I lamented to Casper. I told him I was apologetic about the fact I was lamenting to him, but in reality I wasn't, not really. He seemed to be listening, his expressions at least accurate for what I was telling him as he continued to eat through his ice cream. Mine was melting in my hand. I licked up the melted ice cream.

"It's shitty," he said. I looked at him over my ice cream. "All of it. Every bit of it. I mean, *yes* I want more details about the fact you were sleeping with a teacher. Like, what the fuck, but Cassidy, this isn't the end of the world," he said.

I shook my head. "It could be for Finn."

"Devon sounds like someone who's all mouth and no trousers."

"What do mean?"

"I *mean*, I don't think he's going to tell anyone. I mean, sure, he told Kennedy, but he's your brother and if

I've been listening to the story correctly, his ex. If he wanted to impact you, he'd have gone straight to the principal." He paused. "At least I would've."

I rose my eyebrow at him. He laughed.

"I get that all this is shitty, Cassidy, but don't let it ruin your week…" He looked at me. "Today."

I nodded softly.

"*And* in regards to the money," he continued, "welcome to my world, Queen."

"Sorry." I winced; he shook his head, amused as he finished his cone.

"Don't be. We'll think of this like an opportunity for a life lesson. You're going to spend the day like poor little me," he relished in saying.

I frowned at him then shook my head. "What do you mean?"

"We're going to survive the day on twenty pounds."

"Impossible," I said in a breath. "There wouldn't even be enough to drink with later."

"That's why we work, sweetie," he said, then lifted my chin with his finger. "And I know princesses like you haven't worked a day in your life. Let's get our hands dirty."

I crinkled my nose at him. He laughed, taking my hand in his.

"Not literally," he assured me, lifting my hand up between us. "We're not going to ruin those nails. Nuh-huh."

"I am developing feelings for you," I told him. He laughed.

"First thing we're going to do is lunch." He nodded to me. I frowned but silently agreed. "And you're going to meet my friends."

"I'm… *what*?"

"You need to spend this afternoon around people who don't know you," he said, lifting his first finger, "and my friends are the best."

"We've all said that about our best friends."

"Yeah, but mine are *actually* the best," he said. I laughed as he got his phone out, still pulling me forward as he sent a text.

He stopped when his phone dinged in his hand, changing our direction.

"So, one of the musical theatre modules is that they have to audition and perform in a musical."

"Oh my god," I moaned. "Why did I go to Ravenwood?"

"Don't worry, I've been asking myself that question since I met you," he said, smiling. "Basically we have a big lunch because it's…"

"Two-show day. I know."

"Oh he *knows*," he teased. I smiled at my feet. "Well, Nick and I also work tonight."

"Oh, the reason why we couldn't go on a date," I said.

He grinned. "I'm impressed that you're already making a joke about it."

"It's how I hide my pain," I replied. He smiled, pulling me towards him, wrapping his arm over my shoulders then turning us down another street to a part of London I didn't think I'd ever been to before. Every building on the street was a different colour. Lightbulbs hung overhead, rafter to rafter. There was an instrument shop and a vinyl shop. A bookshop and a coffee shop.

"I love this street," I told Casper. He looked at me then began to shake my shoulders.

"This is *my* London," he said then laughed. "We're in artist territory."

"Why do I feel like everyone's about to break out in song?" I whispered.

He laughed. "How I wish."

"The feelings are just growing, Cas," I told him. He grinned at me as he opened a door. The noise from the inside exploded out of it.

"Ah, Casper," the waiter said.

"You're known."

"Shhh," Casper said, putting his finger on my lips. "Is everyone here?"

"Most of them. Usual table, usual order?"

"You know it. My…" He looked at me. "Cassidy will be needing a menu."

The waiter passed me one, winking at me then letting us go. Casper weaved us through the tables perfectly until he came to three tables pushed together. There were boys stood all around it talking animatedly, laughing and playing with each other.

"You're the Queen," one said. I looked towards him then smiled as I recognised him as Nick.

"You're Nick," I told him.

He gasped, touching his chest. "I *am*, whoa," he

added, turning to look at the boy next to him, so I also did. He appeared shy, hiding his laugh behind his hand, but his face was soft, his eyes kind. "Did you know that?"

"Peak sarcasm," the boy said. Nick pulled his tongue at him. The boy laughed. "The Queen, I've heard of the Queen." He almost sang to me. I wanted to curl up in his voice.

"I'm sure," I said. The boy smirked at me.

"Cassidy, right? Cassidy Bradford – ew, you go to Ravenwood."

"Ew, you go to Goldstein," I said. He gasped.

"You're outnumbered here, Queen; we all go to Goldstein," he whispered to me.

I heard a laugh so I turned.

"Excuse me, *I'm* an adult," a man with dark hair and eyes said. I examined him for a little while.

"That's Nick's boyfriend," Casper told me. I turned back to the boy.

"Thomas," I said, then, "oh my god, you're Thomas McNally." He blushed. "Your reputation precedes you," I told him; he hid his face in Nick's shoulder. "How are you so shy? Have you heard yourself sing? You're like, *oh my god* I don't even have the words to describe you."

"Thank you," Nick said, dramatically shaking Thomas's shoulders. "I told you, you were awesome."

"Shut up," Thomas murmured into Nick's shoulder. I laughed then turned.

"So I guess that makes you Harley Railton," I guessed. The blonde-haired green-eyed boy grinned at me.

"Cassidy," he nodded to me, "you're a pretty big deal."

"Me? How about you? I've stumbled upon your TikTok a good few times."

"No likes?"

"Excuse me, the Queen always likes," I said. Harley laughed. "I don't quite know who you are," I said to the man.

He laughed. "I'm not offended, the theatre blogs aren't alight with me," he said, raising his eyebrow at me. I smirked. "Max," he added.

"The ballet dancer, Cameron's boyfriend," I added, then turned back to Casper who had reached his hand out to who could only be his twin brother.

"Huh, is this how people feel when they meet Kennedy and me?" I asked.

Casper laughed. "I guess so, this is…"

"Cam," I said, then bit my lip. "Sorry, a bit too overfamiliar. Cameron. You're Casper's twin."

"And you're the person Casper won't stop talking about," he said.

Casper sighed into his hand. "You're embarrassing."

"It's my job," he said, shrugging, then grinned at me. "I hear you guys met because you were shit-talking me."

"Very true," I confirmed, "but you've got to be good to get on my radar," I added with a shrug then waved the menu at Casper. "What's good to eat here?" I asked, catching as Cameron looked wide-eyed towards Harley.

"I always go for the burger," Casper told me with a nod, "sweet potato chips and lemonade."

"Well…" I said, turning towards the waiter who'd approached us, "I'll have what he has." The waiter nodded, amused, turning on his heel and heading back the way he came. I grinned at Casper as he nodded to me, then turned as every person around me was unified in saying:

"Zack!"

"*Zack,* I assume," I said, then coughed. "Are *all* Goldstein boys attractive? What the fuck."

"Hey," Zack said, amused, offering me his hand. I shook it.

"Never let go," I said softly. He grinned at me before in fact letting go and shaking Thomas's arm.

"Sorry I'm late," he told him. "Rehearsal was *manic,*" he said, then kissed his cheek. "They're recasting Link for anyone who that might be of interest to."

"Link?" I repeated.

"Larkin," Cameron said. I frowned at him. "Zack is a swing in *Hairspray.*"

"Whoa."

"He's one of the Nicest Kids in Town," Thomas obviously mocked; Zack pushed him away, laughing.

"Says you…" he said, grabbing for Thomas's head. He instantly began to laugh, hitting him away. "You're fighting for a cause, but you're *really,* really nice."

"Foods up," the waiter stated, balancing far too many plates with burgers on his arms. "Sweet potato, sweet potato."

"New pet name for us hey, Xander?" Harley said.

The waiter, Xander, hit the back of his head.

"Chicken," he stated, putting said burger in front of Harley. "Vegetarian patty for Zack, more sweet potato for the twins," he said, placing Cameron's then Casper's plate down, "and sweet potato for the newbie."

"It's strange hearing someone else being called the twins," I told Casper, who smirked at me.

"It's strange enough with us, we're not usually within the proximity of each other to be referred to as the twins."

"And, you know the waiter, right?" I asked Harley.

He nodded. "He's my brother," Harley said, smirking towards Xander who laughed as he threw some ketchup sachets onto the table.

"I'm working the tables until I can become a star," he said, putting on a southern drawl. "Mama wants me to look after the baby," he added, wrapping his arms around Harley and kissing his cheeks over and over.

"Go away," Harley moaned, pushing him away with a laugh.

"You should appreciate him; he'll be on the cruise ship before you know it," Cameron said, pointing a chip at him. Harley laughed, shaking his head and taking the salt from me.

"Cruise ship?" I repeated.

Casper nodded. "He and his boyfriend have got a contract with a cruise ship from next January. Entertainers."

"That's so cool," I said. "I know. Some of the performances I've seen on cruise ships have been amazing too."

153

"Performances?" Nick said.

"Plural?" Cameron asked.

I looked around the table. "We've cruised a lot," I said, shrugging, then jumping when they all made siren noises at me.

"Rich kid alert," Nick declared; I covered my mouth as Casper rose his eyebrow at me.

"But where did you go?" Harley whispered to me.

"New York," I answered. They all collectively lost their breath. "The Bahamas, Florida. I've done a lot of Europe, too."

"You guys should've started dating sooner, you might've gotten on some of these trips," Nick said.

I shook my head. "Father would *never*," I said, before turning back to Casper who was scowling at Nick. "I didn't know we were *dating*."

"Oh my god," Casper moaned. "I'm going to kill you."

"I didn't say I *minded*," I added. He looked at me. "In fact, I'd have been pretty pissed if this wasn't a date."

"He's so outspoken. I love and envy him," Thomas said in a sigh. Nick kissed his cheek.

"You should be more so, sweetheart," I told him. Thomas shook his head. I laughed. "Me and my friends literally lapped up your performance as the Genie, what? Two years ago, was it?"

"I only got the role because *he* tore some ligaments in his leg," he said accusingly towards Harley, who nodded to confirm that fact.

"But that role was made for *you*," I stated. "The

moment Noah uploaded it, I told him straight up I wanted more."

Thomas blushed furiously as he shook his head.

"And then he uploaded your Shrek performance, oh my god," I said. Harley smiled at me as I dramatically shook my head.

"Always thought the Ravens hated us?" Cameron said. I shrugged.

"I'd be one of you if my father wasn't a benefactor of Ravenwood. Kennedy…" I paused as Nick and Casper both threw a napkin at me. "*Kennedy* and I were so ready to go to Goldstein when we found out about it. I can secretly stan you all."

"I can't work out if he's just trying to gain favour, or if he's actually genuine," Harley whispered.

"I'm nothing if I'm not genuine," I told him, "but I can stop if it's embarrassing you."

"Oh, now I never said that," he said. "I envy you too by the way. I saw your Anne Boleyn at Christmas, your outfit was *flawless*. The entire dress, your face, *everything*. It was almost as if the entire character was destined for you."

"You're sweet," I told him. He too blushed. "This burger is *incredible*, by the way," I told Casper, who nodded, almost frowning at me.

"Of course it is. Why do you think we're regulars?"

"The price," Xander said as he put the bill on the table.

"Oh how are we, you know, doing this?" I asked. Casper smirked at me as Nick laughed, getting his wallet out of his jeans and putting a ten pound note down.

"My turn to pay for Thomas this week," he said.

"I'm covering Cam," Max said, putting his own note down. Cameron shook his head almost instantly, until Max caught him and kissed him.

"Sad single," Harley announced, raising his fingers into a peace sign as he put five pounds on the table.

"No way."

"Yes way," Casper said. "Burger, chips and a drink, fiver."

"And it tastes *this* good."

"Right?" Xander said as he leant on Harley's chair. "Where's my tip?"

"Well within our twenty-pound budget," Casper said as I put my own note down.

"Okay, okay fine, you've proved your point with lunch, but what are we going to do this afternoon, with just fifteen pounds remaining?"

"Harley," Casper said. Harley nodded to him. "I believe it's the turn of your musical this afternoon."

"Indeed it is Cas, I've been waiting for you to come and see me in the bright lights of Jamie," Harley said dramatically. I hit Casper's arm.

"You're in *Everybody's Talking About Jamie*?"

"I am," Harley said in a laugh.

"Okay, great guru, how are we going to see a West End show for under fifteen pounds? Unless you have free tickets, of course?" I asked Harley. He shook his head.

"Oh," Cameron said, almost tutting at me, "you

know there's seats *behind* the stalls, right?"

"Course, the royal box," I mocked. Cameron rose his eyebrow at me. "I don't think your brother likes me very much," I added to Casper who elbowed Cameron in the stomach.

"I think my brother needs to stop peacocking," Casper stated, then looked at me. "We'll go to the Theatre Bookings box, get some thirteen-pound tickets for the grand circle. Okay?"

"They exist?"

"Wow," I said as I followed Casper down the stairs of the Grand Circle towards our seats. He turned back to look at me, his expression amused, before he lowered the seat he was stood in front of.

"I guess you've never been up *this* high then?"

"No," I said in a gasp as I stood in front of the seat next to him, looking down at the stage.

"This was the only way Cam and I could get to the theatre when we were smaller. We loved it, every time. The first time I sat in the stalls was *Mormon*, when we went to see Thomas, and that was just because he had free tickets."

"I know I'm spoilt," I said as I sat beside him.

He shook his head. "I didn't mean…"

"No, no I *know* you didn't mean that, but I know I am. I'm insanely lucky, but my father does work hard, so hard that he values work over his family. He never took us to the theatre. Sure, he bought the tickets, he got us the best seats and he got the car to pick us up and take us, but he never came."

"What about your mum?" he asked softly.

I looked at him. "She doesn't really like musicals. I adore the woman, don't get me wrong, but it was mostly Kennedy's and my thing. I remember once Harrison, my big brother, and his then boyfriend Preston, bought us tickets to go and see *Aladdin*; we were only five, maybe six, and we were so excited. Preston loved theatre; he was so deeply passionate about it.

"He spent most of the interval telling us little random facts about the show, sharing chocolate buttons with us and playing with us. It was one of the best times."

"They're not together now, I assume?" he asked.

I shook my head slowly. "Preston… Preston died."

"Oh, I'm sorry."

I shook my head. "It's okay. Well, it's not, but you know it kind of is. He always got it; he wanted to be a Golden Boy too, but apparently his voice was only okay and he mustn't have had the piano grades or something… I don't know."

"There's only a handful of pianists a year because each year basically creates an orchestra. He probably didn't get in because there was already a pianist, not because he wasn't good enough."

"I kind of wish someone could've told him that," I said. He met my eyes so I shook my head. "Before this gets too sad, because this is a date, right?"

"Nick I swear, he's the worst best friend," he said, rubbing his head. I knocked my elbow against his.

"Right, right, so you *don't* want this to be a date?"

"I never said *that*," he replied, his voice high pitched.

I smiled at him. "Oooh, you like me," I teased, poking at his sides.

He laughed, reaching for my hands until he could grab them. "Busted," he whispered, his eyes widening at me before he pointed towards the stage, his finger moving to his mouth. "Shh, the show's about to start."

"Okay… you told me something about *your* theatre experiences, here's one of mine," Casper said softly as he came to sit back next to me. He'd stood up pretty quickly when the interval had begun, excusing himself to the bathroom, but returning with a little tub of ice cream. He tore the top off, licking the underside as he sat back next to me. "We were by no means poor, right. We were okay, comfortable I guess. We went to the Winter Gardens mostly, but sometimes we travelled to Liverpool and went to the Empire, or Manchester to the Opera House. Now *that* was exciting." He smiled as I laughed.

"Mum would buy Cam and I a programme to share, and then in the interval an ice cream to share." He lifted the little tub to me. "We *never* complained because we knew things in the theatre usually cost a little more, or they'd already paid so much for the tickets – mostly we were just happy to be there, so we shared the little wooden spoon and the ice cream during the interval." He ate the ice cream off the spoon before holding it to me. I took it from him, grinning lightly as I scooped up some ice cream of my own.

"I guess you spent most of your time in the West

End, right?"

"No," I replied. He seemed surprised as I passed the spoon back. "Only if there was a show that wasn't touring that we wanted to see did we come to the West End. Mostly we went to the Theatre Royal…"

"Which is where?"

"Brighton," I said with a laugh.

"You're from Brighton?"

"Hove, actually," I stated.

He rose his eyebrow as he passed the spoon back. "I assumed you came from London."

"No," I said softly. "The far gayer capital."

"Suddenly, it makes far more sense," he said, then tilted the tub towards me. "The last scoop."

"Oh," I said, dramatically placing my hand on my chest. "This is as good as a proposal."

"I'm glad I'm living up to your standards."

We walked back to his boarding house when we left the theatre, as he'd told me he needed to pick up his trumpet. His boarding house wasn't quite as grand as mine. The walls were painted a dark blue, the carpet plush under our feet, and we ran, hand in hand past door after door until he had to fish his student card out of his pocket.

He glanced at me as he beeped us through the door. I snatched his card from his hand, lifting it out of his reach to look at it.

"Cute," I told him, "but not as cute as I'd hoped. I wanted you to be eleven with braces and freckles."

He shook his head, amused, trying to reach up for his

card. "I've never had braces."

"Lucky," I said, nodding.

"Wait," he said as he finally retrieved his card. I walked ahead of him. "You had braces?"

I turned back to look at him, raising my finger to my lips. He smirked, walking past me, and beeped open a door. He held it open for me as I stepped in. There were five beds in the room, and *no* people. I glanced at him.

"We're roomed with our section, so brass room one," he said, then pointed at the nearest bed. "Trombone." The next bed. "Saxophone." Next bed. "Second trumpet." He smiled. "Tuba, and then…" He sat on the last bed.

"First trumpet?" I suggested. He nodded. "Which is Nick?"

"Drums," he said, tilting his head at me, "in the percussion room."

"You're not in the same room as your best friend? How does that work?"

"Well, I sleep in here."

"No, no," I said, laughing, then went to sit on the end of his bed. He nodded to me. "I board too. Your best friend is the boy on the bed next to you."

"I mean sure," he said, amused, "but no, these boys are pretty cool and I can talk to them, and being here of a night isn't bad, but no. I met Nick first when we arrived. His dad was dropping him off at the entrance whilst my dad was dropping me off, Mum dropping Cam at the theatre campus. We basically stuck to each other, because I saw him first; we found our rooms together, went to eat together."

"Seven years later, you're still best friends?"

"Yeah," he smiled. I looked away from him as I also smiled.

"What do you have planned for me this evening?" I asked. He smirked at me.

Thirteen

We walked to what looked like a coffee shop but could've been *anything*, sharing a cone of chips between us that we'd bought earlier with one of our last four pounds. We stood outside until we finished them.

The door dinged as we walked in.

The man behind the till looked up at the ding, smiling brightly.

"Casper, you're early."

"Well I've brought a new victim…" He coughed. "Volunteer."

I laughed, shaking my head as I followed Casper to the counter. The man was young, really not that much older than us. He had multiple pride pins on his apron, and his name, Hunter, written onto his badge.

"Who is our new volunteer, huh?"

"Cassidy," Casper and I said together. The man rose his eyebrow.

"Golden Boy?"

"Oh no, Raven," Casper said, sending a playful snarl in my direction. I rolled my eyes dramatically.

"Wow, we don't often have Ravens in here, let me get the fancy china," he teased, winking at me. "So, are you going to sing?" he added. Casper looked at me as I bit my lip.

"Well, *are* you?"

"I don't know," I admitted. "Does everyone?"

"If you want to drink, *yes*." Casper shrugged. "Eating, too; sometimes you can get food out of it."

"Depending how good you are," Hunter said with a laugh.

"This is a bar?"

"Yeah, bar and food. With live music on a Friday and Saturday."

"How do you make a profit?" I asked.

Hunter laughed as he retrieved two menus and a wooden spoon, proceeding to lead us to a table. "Not everything is about money, sunshine."

"I'm starting to learn that…" I told him, smiling at Casper as he grinned back. "But a business is."

"You pay me a pound to sing, you keep your tips. Then, people flock in because of your beautiful voices…" He paused. "And trumpet playing. I make far more than I make any other night because of your voices – so I can spare you guys a free sandwich."

"Satisfactory?" Casper asked. I bit my lip as I nodded and took a seat on the armchair. It sunk the moment I sat in it. Casper passed Hunter a pound.

"First up," he told Casper before looking at his watch. "Ten minutes. I'll bring you some water for the table."

I glanced at Casper, then startled as the door dinged again and noise came through – or more precisely, Cameron and his boyfriend Max, and Nick who was barely through the door before he ran to Casper, almost tackling him as he wrapped his arms around him.

"Ow," Casper said in surprise, laughing as he slipped his hand into Nick's jacket, pulling out his drumsticks. "Lethal," he stated as he attempted to twirl the drumsticks around his fingers – it didn't work. Instead, it flew from his hand into my lap.

I picked up the stick in an attempt to offer it back, but got distracted.

"You have engraved drumsticks."

Nick smirked at me as he took the stick off me, successfully twirling it in his fingers.

"They were a gift," he said then pointed them at me. "From—"

"Thomas," Casper finished as the door dinged again. I looked towards it as Thomas stepped through, holding the door open for Harley and Zack. They were all still wearing their stage makeup, their faces practically glowing, but that could've been the smiles on their faces, as they seemed to create an atmosphere with just their presence.

They all gave Hunter a pound, smiling pleasantly at him before joining our table, and then the noise. The chatter, the jokes and the laughter as they told anecdotes of their show day.

"Good evening, everybody," Hunter said, jumping up onto the stage. The room cheered back at him. "I've never been one for speeches, so let's get the drinks flowing. Eat the food whilst its hot and enjoy the live music from my favourite group of Golden Boys. They've even brought a Raven with them tonight, but we don't know yet if he's brave enough to sing." He goaded me; he was *fucking* goading me. The smirk in my direction just proved it. "But in the meantime, Casper, darling. Get us started."

Casper nodded as he stood, unclipping his case and retrieving his trumpet. He winked at me as he stepped onto the stage. He waved, laughing into the microphone as he introduced himself and then he began to play. It was familiar, definitely, and it was beautiful.

I marvelled at how different the sound was from Kennedy's saxophone, but it was just as beautiful, just as expertly played. I had snuck into several of Kennedy's saxophone lessons when we were younger because I enjoyed listening. I adored the sound the saxophone made – or in fact any instrument in the brass section. I could sit and listen to it all night.

"So, I guess you're boyfriends now?" Cameron said, startling me out of listening so intently. I turned to look at him. He was examining me with his eyes.

"Why?" I asked.

"I'm just asking." He shrugged.

"You seem protective of him," I said.

"Did he tell you he was gay?"

"No…" I answered slowly. "He told me he was pan."

"It's all very new to him and…"

"I know. He told me, all about him figuring out his sexuality. It isn't as straightforward to everyone. It was to me, sure. People have been calling me gay since I could talk – it was easy. I guess it was for you, too."

He shrugged lightly. "I guess so, I don't know."

"You never doubted it though, right? You said the word gay and it clicked."

"Yeah," he said.

"It was a little bit more complicated for him," I said, nodding to Casper. "Labels change sometimes, but that doesn't make him vulnerable or, I don't know, in need of protecting."

"He's my brother."

"I know," I stressed. "I know better than most, actually, because I have a twin brother, too. But you know what, it's not my job to keep track of what Kennedy puts his dick in. I just need to know he's happy putting it there."

"What is Casper happy putting his dick in, you?"

"We haven't done that… yet," I said in a laugh, "but I hope so. I know I'll be happy putting mine in *him*." I scrunched my nose. "A bit crude but we'll go with it."

He nodded, looking away from me as Casper changed song.

"How did you guys meet?" I asked, nodding to Max who was laughing with the rest of the group.

"He…" Cameron sighed, sounding content, "he was one of the dancers in *Fame* – I was in *Fame* earlier this year for our module, and he was a dancer. I fell ridiculously head-first in love with him pretty much instantly," he said, looking up at me, so I smiled. "We only really started dating before Christmas, but it feels like forever."

"He's not in school with you?"

"No..." He laughed as Max turned to look at us. "He's twenty-two, he's a ballet dancer."

I met Max's eye as he nodded whilst drinking from his glass.

"You're twenty-two?" I repeated. Cameron turned to look at him as Max laughed.

"I am. I don't just choose to hang out with teenagers, honest," he added. I laughed then turned as Casper drew his song to its end. We all applauded loudly, wooting and hitting the tables as he took his bow. Hunter applauded as he lifted the microphone from behind the till.

"Always a pleasure, Casper," he said as Casper sat back beside me. "A certain Mr Nicolas Redgrave is called to the stage," he continued. Nick laughed as he stood, twirling his drumsticks as he walked to the drum set at the back of the stage.

"You're pretty good at that trumpet," I told Casper, who smirked as he knocked our shoulders together.

"Do you really think so?" he asked, batting his eyelashes at me. I smirked as he laughed, lifting his drink to me with a nod. For unaccompanied drums it wasn't all too unpleasant to just listen to, it wasn't loud and chaotic as one would expect drums to be. It was soft and musical and perfect; that was until he played the beginning of

'Friend Like Me', a little smirk in our direction, making Casper jump out of his seat like a whippet, getting his trumpet and running up on stage with him.

"This is why they're best friends," Thomas said, nodding as he sat on the seat next to me. "They're bad influences on each other."

"I thought those were the rules of best friends."

He looked towards Zack.

"True. What's your best friend like?" he asked. I glanced at him as he shrugged. "Or don't you have best friends? Do you just have *followers*?"

"You know…" I said slowly, "I don't know." I whispered because right now who *was* my best friend? Finn? My *teacher*? That didn't seem right. There was Cody but he was Kennedy's best friend, nee Stephen of course. I'd *always* said it was Theo – but where was he now? Where had he even been the last few weeks? Disappearing off around corners or slipping away unseen.

"That just upset me," he said. "I'll be your new best friend." He sounded serious, so I laughed then I shook my head.

"Zack might have something to say about that."

Thomas laughed. "He *is* very sensitive, it's true."

"You're talking about me, aren't you?" Zack asked, looking our way. We both waved. He rolled his eyes.

"From what I can tell you're one of the most popular in Ravenwood."

"I am," I confirmed. "I'm the Queen," I added with a flare.

He rose his eyebrow at me. "I guess it's lonelier at the top than expected."

"Erm, excuse me," Nick said over the microphone. We both turned towards him. "I'm going to need some vocals for this next one." I looked back at Thomas as he began to shake his head. "Yep," Nick said simply. Thomas sighed then looked at me.

"What are you waiting for?" I said. He looked a little wide-eyed. "Go and own that stage, you've got a voice to do so."

"Really?" he whispered. I nodded as he bit his lip then sighed and stood, stepping up onto the stage, shaking his head at Nick who grinned, passing him over the microphone. Thomas hid behind the microphone shaking his head, his cheeks reddening as Nick began to play the beat. Casper knocked his elbow against Thomas, winking at him before joining in with his trumpet. Thomas took a breath out, and then he began to sing.

"Oh my god," I whispered.

"Yep," Cameron said from beside me. I looked at him. "That's Thomas. Doesn't look you in the eye when he talks to you, but can hold an entire room's attention with just his voice."

"It's a skill," Harley said, "*and* somewhat attractive."

We all murmured in agreement and then we laughed softly so not to disturb his singing.

He bowed shyly when the room gave a thunderous applause. He laughed, turning to Nick and whispering to him. Nick nodded almost instantly.

"I'm not doing this one alone," Thomas said into the

microphone. He rose his eyebrow expectantly, but it didn't take long. Zack laughed as he stood and joined Thomas on the stage. Cameron followed, shaking his head dramatically but taking up position next to him.

Harley stopped just before he got onto the stage.

"Well come on," he said, holding his hand out to me. "I'm pretty sure you'll know this one. If you don't, I want you to give up your theatre card and never step foot in the theatre again." I bit my lip then nodded, taking his hand and letting him pull me onto the stage. I knew it the moment it started, so I grinned at Harley who winked back at me, then rose the microphone and we began to sing.

"You're staying on this stage, by the way," Harley told me as he stepped off.

"What?" I said in a laugh, holding the microphone out to him. He shook his head, holding his hands away from me, so I turned to Thomas who also shook his head.

"It's time to prove why you're the Queen," Zack stated. "I want to know if the rumours are true."

"Oh," I said simply, as Casper also jumped from the stage.

"Think of it as initiation," Cameron said, so I nodded, licking my lips then clearing my throat.

"Okay, well I'm going to take this away from musicals for a second..." I paused. "Which I know is sacrilege, but bear with me."

"Just tell me what you want, Queen," Nick said.

I hadn't sung in *so* long.

Not really anyway. Finn didn't ask me to audition anymore — my reputation preceded me — and I hardly sang in the theatre. I hadn't even sung for fun for almost a year, given how much work goes into our Christmas Showcase. I had been singing 'Don't Lose Your Head' on repeat from July through December. It felt nice not to be and it felt good watching up close people who'd never seen me perform. Except Casper; I didn't look at Casper.

I lowered the microphone.

The power of the applause almost sent me back a few steps, and I laughed.

"Well, I guess you can keep your crown," Harley said, so I blew him a kiss.

I stood outside the bar after a few drinks and a sandwich that deserved more credit than anyone was giving it. I leant my head back against the bricks, blowing the smoke upwards.

"You smoke."

I jumped.

"*That's* a bad habit."

I laughed.

"Judging is a bad habit, too," I told Casper as he smirked, leaning on the wall beside me.

"On a scale of one to ten, how well do you think today on twenty pounds went?"

"Depends," I said softly, looking at him as I held my cigarette at my side.

"On?"

"How much a kiss will eat into our budget."

"Oh," he said, amused, then reached for the cigarette. I let him take it, raising my eyebrow at him as he inhaled some. "I guess that's within budget," he whispered, pulling me towards him and kissing me.

He smirked at me when he pulled back but not too far. I laughed then kissed him again.

Fourteen

There were whispers. All around me. I wasn't listening to them, not really, but I was more tuned into them than whatever my English teacher was trying to teach us. I glanced back towards Cody's desk, seeing as he frowned whilst continuing to tear at a piece of paper on his desk.

He met my eyes.

I tilted my head at him.

He shrugged.

I tuned in.

"I can't believe it…"

"Is it true?"

"It can't be. I mean, *sure*, he's been with loads of people, but that's a bit far, right…"

"Did you see who it was?"

"The picture's dark, it was hard to tell."

"The Queen, really…"

I sat up a little better, straightening my blazer then

raising my hand. My English teacher, god love her, called on me pretty much instantly.

"I just wanted to say," I told her. She nodded to me, practically hanging on every word that came out my mouth – sometimes I forget just how much power I have over this school.

"If you're *going* to be talking about me, at least say it loud enough that I can hear the rumour. Thanks. Please continue with your thrilling lesson." I glanced around the room, watching as the rest of my class sat aptly chastised before looking at Cody, who applauded me gently.

I went to find Archie in my break.

He was, as predicted, stood outside my locker reading from a glossy magazine.

"What's this?" I asked, pointing at the magazine in his hand. He sighed, turning it to me. I laughed. "Wow, front page, I'm honoured," I said as I saw a picture of me in the bottom corner of the magazine. I brought it closer.

Potential Prime Minister's son gay?

"Why is there even a question mark?" I muttered, then flicked through the magazine as *apparently* I could read more on page six. Which I could, as there was a half-page picture of me and Casper, except it was just the back of Casper, *my* cigarette between his fingers as he spoke to me and I smiled like an idiot.

The picture next to it was of us kissing.

I sighed.

"Who is it?" Archie whispered. I looked at him as he stuttered, "you don't have to tell me... I mean..."

"Boyfriend... I think," I answered. Archie looked

surprised, then he trained his face. "Don't worry, I'm surprised, too," I added, smiling at him he looked away. "This was our first kiss, so I *love* that invasion of privacy. I'm just glad they weren't whispering about Finn," I added in a sigh, looking down the corridor and landing on Devon as he stood mostly hidden by his locker.

"Finn?" Archie repeated. I glanced at him. He rose his eyebrow back at me. "I'm going to jump to my own conclusions… and enjoy them."

"You do that, sweetheart," I said, amused. "Thank you. If you hear anything keep me updated."

"Of course," he said, scanning his eyes over the corridor, "and any rumours will be shut down. You have my word."

"I love you, you know," I told him. He blushed, burying his face into the collar of his blazer as I grinned at him.

I *really* hoped Archie wasn't my best friend. As much as I loved him, of course, and as much as he obviously loved me, he was just fourteen and it wasn't good for my street cred if a fourteen-year-old was my best friend – god.

I looked down the corridor, focusing on Devon for longer than he deserved before my eyes landed on Theo as he swapped the books in his locker.

"Thank you, Archie, for real," I said. He nodded before walking around me to his own locker.

I went to Theo's.

"You're famous."

"Always have been," I said as I leant on the locker

next to him. He glanced at me. "Who are you sleeping with?"

"Who are *you* sleeping with?" He laughed. "Well, besides Finn…" he added, raising his eyebrow at me. I narrowed my eyes at him. "I can't believe I didn't figure that out," he said as he closed his locker. "It was so glaringly obvious."

"How do you know now?"

He turned, briefly looking down towards Devon. I pushed myself from the locker.

"Seriously?" I said. He shrugged as I pushed past him, crowding Devon at his locker. He turned to look at me, his eyes widening as I pushed him back against his locker.

"What have you been whispering?" I hissed at him.

He shook his head. "Nothing."

I frowned at him. "Are you scared of me?"

"I…" he began. I pulled him towards me, further into the light. He looked small, as if he was pulling himself in. I'd never seen Devon look so tiny, so afraid, his arrogance gone.

There was a dark purple bruise under his left eye.

"Who hit you?" I asked. He shook his head. "*Who*, Devon?"

"Kennedy," he spat at me. "He came after me and he did this, okay? He told me not to even *think* about telling anyone what I knew – but you did that all by yourself, didn't you? The front of a magazine, huh? Future prime minister's son, gay? I think that's a bit of an understatement for you."

"It's not Finn," I said through gritted teeth.

He shook his head. "What does it matter now?" he spat back. I shook my head. "Finn won't get fired. Your dad will be elected because, look now, he has a diversity vote and with two, *two* months left in this school I've been kicked out of the choir."

"You've been…"

"So there's no point, Cassidy." He pushed me back.

"Devon…" I said.

He shook his head, slamming his locker shut. "Leave me alone, Cassidy."

"Devon," I repeated, reaching for his wrist, holding it tight in my hand. He stopped but didn't look at me. "When we went to the theatre, I actually *wanted* to be your friend. We had a good night, I enjoyed being with you. You're better than all this blackmail and schemes."

He shook his head.

"In two months, you can start again. Leave all this shit behind and do exactly what you want to do. This shit won't stick to you forever."

He turned back to look at me so I sighed. "Why are you saying this?"

"Because no one deserves to feel worthless or alone. *Ever.*"

"I could've ruined your life."

"Not mine, *no*. Finn's, yeah. That'd have been bad but you didn't."

"I was going to."

"But you *didn't*," I said. He looked at our shoes. "Just go quiet. Okay? Do the last two months with your head down. Just get through them."

"Okay," he whispered, then pulled his wrist out of my grip. I let him, raising my hands as he began to walk away from me.

"Why are you giving *him* the time of day?" Kennedy said from behind me. I looked at him when he was stood next to me, then I lifted his fist. It was mildly bruised.

"I think we're even," I told him then I shook my head. "No more, okay?" I added, stroking over his knuckles before reaching into my pocket for my vibrating phone.

Father is Calling…

"Besides, I think we've got bigger problems."

"You were photographed," Father said, throwing the magazine down onto his desk. I didn't break his stare. "With a *boy*, in the cheapest area of London. What do you think that does for my image?"

"Oh," I said. He looked up at me, anger clear in his expression. "I figured it made you look slightly more human, you know, down to earth, not above the people who are supposedly voting for you."

"Cassidy," he growled. I shrugged. "With a boy…"

"Shocker, I'm gay," I replied. He shook his head. "It's not like I was having anal sex with him up against the wall. We were talking, we were smiling and laughing and then we kissed – nothing else. Which is no different to, *oh* look, *this* photo," I said, turning the page and slamming the magazine back onto his desk on a picture of a minor celebrity and her boyfriend.

"You tipped off the press," he said.

I laughed. "Oh no, no, if I'd tipped off the press there wouldn't be a question mark after that headline."

"You are infuriating," he stated.

I laughed. "What do you want me to do? Not meet people, not go out? I'm sorry I'm not in a perfect relationship like Harrison and Dom that you can hide with ease. What *is* Dom to the press? The childminder, was it? The nanny, not the husband, and I mean let's not even talk about Kennedy and Stephen."

"Cassidy, it is far more complicated than you realise."

"Homophobia rarely is," I said. He hit his desk. I almost jumped.

"We have to deal with this in an appropriate way. I can't come off bad in this situation, so I have set up a date…"

I laughed. "Excuse me?"

"I have heeded advice and it'd look poor on my part if I told the press you aren't gay. I'll come off…" He shook his head as he rubbed his forehead. "Anyway, I was advised to send you on a date, address the rumours, confirm that you're…"

"Gay," I helped, then shook my head. "What about Casper?"

"Casper?"

"The boy in the photo," I said.

He shook his head. "He is irrelevant."

"Oh, please, ensure you lead with that when you meet him."

"Cassidy," he growled; I rolled my eyes. "This date,

he's a nice young man, son of one of my MPs. Very well respected, graduating from Oxford this year."

"He sounds *such* fun," I told him. He met my eyes with a cold stare. I sighed. "Who is he?"

"David Medlock."

"Oh," I said, because *ohhh*. I'd slept with him last year at an event, or a grand lunch or *something* that required me to wear a suit. "I want to be with Casper. I don't want to go on a fake date."

"You don't have to like him."

"Wow," I replied, "is that your approach to dating all the time? Or…"

"Cassidy," he said, but it came out less of a warning, more like a negotiation was coming. I narrowed my eyes at him. "If you do this for me, if you help me out, I'll reinstate your allowance."

"What?" I whispered.

He nodded. "No questions asked. I will start putting your allowance back into your bank every month like before. Do we have a deal?" he asked.

Fifteen

The party was *loud*. Louder than any party had been this year. It was in one of the choir's houses; they'd obviously thrown it in an effort to regain some sort of status – it wasn't working, not really, as all the choir seemed to be acting like cats on heat.

Devon was nowhere to be seen.

Neither was Theo come to think of it.

I'd arrived with Kennedy, but we'd arrived late – partly because I'd stood in our bathroom persuading myself that I wanted to go to this party. I still wasn't one hundred percent on the decision to arrive. Kennedy had disappeared off into Stephen's arms pretty much the moment we'd stepped through the door, and now I was stood alone with half a cup full of vodka.

"Hey, Queen."

I turned then rose my eyebrow at Rowan as he began to make his own drink.

"Been hearing loads of whispers about you, you know," he said conversationally.

"Anything good?" I asked.

He looked at me, shrugging as he sipped from his drink. "That your latest flame is a Golden Boy." I frowned at him, but he continued. "And I thought, things couldn't be *that* bad for you, right? That you have to go *there*."

"Why exactly do you think you're above them?"

"What?" he said laughing. "We are. We've beat them every year."

"Actually, *we* haven't done anything, the orchestra has beaten them."

"When did you become such a bitch?"

"When I stopped judging people, I guess," I said. Rowan scoffed, going to walk away from me, so I reached out for him. "How did you know?"

"About what?" he practically spat at me.

"That Cas is a Golden Boy?"

"Theo told me," he said with a shrug. I frowned at him. "Didn't really know whether to believe it after he told us all you were apparently shagging Finn, but come on, *he's* not that desperate."

I laughed. He looked taken back.

"Fuck you, Rowan," I said, shaking my head and turning on my heels, searching through the other rooms of the house.

"Hey," I said loud enough that a few of the theatre boys near to me turned to look. "Have any of you seen Theo?"

"He went upstairs," Lucah said. I turned towards him.

"With someone?" I asked. Lucah nodded, frowning at me as I went to leave.

"Cassidy," he said. I stopped. "Is it true your boy's a Golden Boy?"

"Does it matter if he is?"

He shrugged lightly at me before looking into his cup of whatever alcohol he was drinking. I rolled my eyes as I left the room, taking the stairs two at a time, bypassing the line as long as the hallway for the bathroom. I pushed open the first bedroom door I reached, leaving it open behind me when I didn't find Theo, ignoring the shouts that told me to close the door again.

He wasn't behind the second or third door either. He was behind the fourth, sat on the big double bed putting his clothes back on.

"What the fuck have you been telling people about me?"

He looked up, surprised, frowning at me as he stood from the bed.

"What?" he said in a laugh.

I shook my head. "Don't you fucking laugh this off, you've been telling people all kinds about me and I want to know why."

"None of it has been a lie," he stated.

I shook my head at him. "What's going on, Theo?"

"Wait, you actually *are* sleeping with Finn?"

I turned, looking behind him, then I laughed. "Marley," I said, then turned back to Theo. "Marley, *he's* who all this has been about, all the secrets, the little notes and lovesick smiles. Marley."

"You slept with him, too, what are you judging for?"

"Judging, *me*, no. You can have my seconds, whatever, I hope you're both fucking happy living your domestic gay life, *after* you've told me why you're spreading things about me."

"I'm just telling people the facts. Your stupid fling with Finn that you thought, what, would get you ahead? Would make you the best in the theatre? Did you get what you wanted?"

"You don't know a thing about my relationship with Finn, don't even for a second pretend that you do. Just because you're jealous of me, doesn't make it okay to act like I didn't earn it."

"Yeah, must've been real hard bending over for him."

"Fuck you," I shouted at him, pushing him back. He stumbled backwards, falling onto the bed. "I hope you've got a spare bed, Marley, because you are not welcome in our room tonight," I told Theo.

"You can't do that," Theo snapped back at me; I shook my head.

"I can do whatever the fuck I like, because I am the *mother*fucking Queen."

I left the room, watching as the crowd of people parted, letting me through, whispering to each other as I passed them.

The entire party watched as I left.

I walked back to the boarding house after unlocking my

phone a few times, as I considered calling Casper and asking where he was.

I decided not to when I'd opened Snapchat and saw that he was performing through Harley's story, but I'd make sure I saw him tomorrow.

"What are you doing out of bed?"

I jumped violently, turning quickly as Finn laughed from where he was stood. He rose his eyebrow at me as he lifted his mug to drink from it. He was obviously on night patrol as he wore a t-shirt from *Waitress* and a pair of joggers, holding his mug, probably coffee.

"Isn't everyone who's anyone at this party tonight?" he asked.

"I thought we couldn't talk anymore." I sighed.

"Queen," he said as I went to push the door to the dorms open. "Cassidy."

I stopped.

"I need to walk through first to fifth. Come with," he suggested. I looked at him as he seemed to examine me.

"Who did you see in *Waitress*?" I asked as I stepped through the door.

He smiled at me as he also stepped through. "Sara Bareilles," he said, then laughed. "Completely by accident. My friend and I, we just booked tickets for a date we could do, turned out that was when she'd taken over the role."

"That's so cool."

"It was amazing. Have you seen it?"

"Multiple times. I dragged Kennedy the first time, and he practically begged me to come the other times," I said as Finn swiped us into the first-year corridor. It was surprisingly quiet. I'd really expected at least some noise coming from somewhere.

"I remember it used to feel like we were breaking the law or something when night patrol walked down and we were still awake."

"When in reality it was only ten o'clock?" he said softly, smirking at me as we continued to follow the corridor. "Why are you back at ten anyway?"

"I…" I began, then shook my head. "Doesn't matter."

"Cassidy…" He sighed.

"I was starting to feel like I didn't belong at that party. Okay?"

"Why not? Aren't parties like *your* thing?"

"Some things came to light," I shrugged as we stepped through to the seconds corridor. Now there was a hive of noise.

"I hate night patrol," Finn muttered. I laughed as he started down the corridor, trying to figure out where the noise was coming from. "There's always *something*, it doesn't matter what day it is," he added, then knocked on the door he was stood by.

The noise fell away. He rolled his eyes at me then he opened the door. He was instantly spoken to, the second years behind the door repeating 'sir' like the seagulls in *Finding Nemo*.

Somehow, he silenced them all.

"You go to the nurse, you and you take his sheets to the laundry and bring new ones back, and yes *Waitress*

187

was amazing."

I laughed, covering my mouth as he took a step back, letting one of the boys out of the room. He stopped in front of me looking wide eyed as his cupped hands became even more covered in blood.

"Go," I said, and he did, almost walking straight into the door. He was saved by another second year who ran past me to open the doors for him. Two more then appeared walking in the other direction with balled-up sheets between them.

Finn sighed, leaning on the door of the room.

"Nosebleed," he said then, "Exciting. What came to light?"

"Betrayal," I said, narrowing my eyes at him.

"How Shakespearean of you."

I shook my head. "I've got a lot to think over."

"If you need to make sense of things you can always come and talk to me."

"Aren't you afraid we might get caught?" I mocked. He frowned at me. He almost looked hurt, so I looked away.

"Cassidy. Any time, whenever that might be, any time you need to talk. I'll be there for you."

"Thank you," I said in a whisper. He nodded. "I'll see you on Monday for rehearsal. Okay?" I asked.

"Stay safe, Cassidy." I started towards the corridor that'd take me back towards my own. I strolled, my hands in my pockets, my phone vibrating against my thigh over and over.

I figured it'd be Kennedy. Maybe Cody. Maybe the

theatre boys' group chat. Either way I didn't want to respond to any of them.

My room was empty when I let myself in. I hadn't expected it any other way. The fairy lights that were draped over mine and Theo's headboards were on, glowing lowly. Something we'd agreed to do last year when we started stumbling into our pitch-black room so drunk we couldn't see straight.

The low glow of the fairy lights was welcoming and warm and not too harsh on the eyes, but also somehow filled the room with enough light for us to navigate.

So I didn't turn on the light.

Instead, I changed out of my clothes into a hoodie and a pair of shorts, picking up my headphones and taking a seat on the windowsill, pressing play on the next chapter of my audio book.

A love story between a wizard and a knight. It was exciting and sweet and somehow the sexiest thing I'd ever witnessed all at the same time.

My eyes wandered as I listened, looking out at the grounds towards the woods. The lights of the grounds didn't stretch as far as the woods – I guess to defer people from going into them, especially of a night, so I focused in on the little glow of light on the edge of the woods.

It wasn't big, not at all; it could've been a phone. It moved around a bit as if it was being used as a torch before it settled nearer to the floor.

I paused the book, watching as the light remained lit, then I stood, putting my phone into my pocket and stepping into my chucks.

It wasn't cold out. The late spring nights were beginning to draw in and, although it still wasn't light, the chill of winter wasn't lingering.

I got out of the school shockingly easily, passing the fifths' corridor and seeing Finn stood in a doorway talking to a room of kids about something.

The grounds on a whole were quiet. I could see some lights on from rooms in the sixth and seventh corridors, of those who hadn't been invited to the party. There was low music coming of one of them. It was so quiet I couldn't hear the words, but the beat sounded soft, almost relaxing.

I continued towards the glowing light.

I stopped a few steps behind the person the glowing light belonged to. They turned it off almost instantly and then we stayed there quiet until he turned to look at me.

"Devon."

He sighed. "What do you want?"

"Well, I saw this glowing light from my window and thought, hey if it's aliens I could be their Queen."

"Why aren't you at…"

"The party?"

"Yeah."

"I was getting kind of bored."

He frowned at me as I shrugged and took a step closer to him.

"I guess the party's over then."

"What?"

"Well, once you leave that's it." He shrugged. "That was how it worked. If you and Kennedy showed up the party was worthy of going ahead, but if either of you left before it was over, that's it."

"Me, *no*. Kennedy, possibly."

"Your opinion was more highly regarded than Kennedy's," he said. I frowned as I sat beside him on the grass. It tickled at my thighs. "You wanted the Queen at your party. It was great to have the King there but that was mostly just because it meant you were on his radar, but if the Queen was there, it meant you were worth his time."

I shrugged. "Well, this one wasn't."

"It was Percy's, wasn't it?"

I nodded. "Why weren't you there?"

"I wasn't invited," he muttered.

I looked down at my shoes. "Why are you here?" I whispered.

He looked away from me. "Percy will be *well* pissed. He only threw this party to get the choir back on people's radars and if *you* left, wow."

"Are you here so you didn't have to be there when they came back?"

"I've been sleeping in the sick room," he said. I frowned as he looked back at me. "My entire room doesn't want to be associated with me."

"I thought they were your friends."

He laughed. "Those gaggle of bitches? Never. They just follow whoever is willing to give them orders. When... when *everything* happened and I was removed from the choir they just stopped talking to me. I lasted a day before I requested I move to the sick room."

"What's the sick room?"

He laughed; I shook my head at him.

"Wait, you're serious?" he said. I shrugged. "It's where you sleep if you're sick, like properly sick. If you need a teacher to be with you."

"Oh."

"I came here to... kill myself," he said weakly. I never dropped my eyes. "I... I figured now was the appropriate time – no one would notice because you were all at a party and I wasn't in their room anyway and it was the weekend."

He looked out towards the trees again, but I didn't look away from him.

"I figured no one would notice."

"Why?" I whispered.

He shook his head. "Why would anyone notice? Everyone hates me, that's what Theo said."

"Theo," I repeated.

He looked down, picking at the grass. "He was who told me about your Golden Boy," he said with a shrug, "and confirmed Finn."

"*What?*" I couldn't believe what I was hearing. Why would Theo do that? I shook my head. "People would notice," I told him.

He shook his head. "Bullshit. No one would notice, no one would *care*."

"I would," I said.

He laughed so loudly it shocked both of us. "You

would not. You're saying that because you feel sorry for me. Which is why I wanted to do this without anyone around because I cannot deal with being pitied."

"I don't pity you," I said. "Not at all. I also don't feel sorry for you, but I am telling you the truth."

"You've never liked me."

"This has got nothing to do with me liking you, or in fact you liking me because I know you've never liked me either, but I have *always* had a level of respect for you."

"Are you ever off?"

"What?"

"Do you stop being the fucking Queen? The oracle, the empathetic well spoken, whatever you are, do you *ever* stop?"

"I…"

"I don't want you here if you're going to talk to me like I'm one of your subjects. I don't want you here at all in fact."

"Fine, you want me to stop?" I said. He looked at me. "I'll stop. Fine. You… you were a dick to me, and to Kennedy. You took his virginity and acted like it didn't mean a thing and I was livid with you. I couldn't believe someone could be *that* self-centred, but you're not a bad person. I know you're not. Why? Because of fucking second year."

He looked at me. "I didn't think you…"

"Of course I remember."

Our residential in second year is a four-day camp. I am not in any way a camper; the four-day experience was literally hell on earth for me. I was put in a tent with

193

Theo as Kennedy was put with Cody, but this was still back when our teachers were trying to persuade us that everyone was your best friend regardless of your interests, so for our adventurous activities during the day they paired us off with whoever came out of the hat.

For caving which involved every single thing I hated.

Small spaces.

Mud. Lots of mud.

The dark.

Small spaces.

And, helmets.

Devon came out of the hat. I begged our supervising teacher, who wasn't Finn for this activity, to let me sit out, to give me a pass. *Please don't make me go down into the cave.*

He told me to *man up* and get down there, and how I resented him, because even as a twelve-year-old, being told to do something I was severely uncomfortable with did not sit right. He told me it was unfair to Devon because *Devon* wanted to do this activity and I was stopping him.

It turned out Devon hated the idea of this activity almost as much as I did, but he daren't mention not wanting to go into that cave. Instead, we got to the mouth of the cave and our helmets secured and Devon held his hand out to me.

"It's dark in there," he said so quietly I almost couldn't hear him — because his voice was breaking and he was choosing not to talk through it. "I don't like the dark."

"I don't like how small it is in there," I told him as I watched the last of the headlights disappear around the corner.

"I'll hold your hand if you hold mine," he offered, "and I won't let go at any point."

"Promise?"

"I promise," he told me, so I held onto his hand, and neither of us let go until we got to the other side, even though it was horrible and I cried for the majority of it.

But Devon never told. He never told a soul that I'd sobbed the moment it got too dark and too small, that he'd squeezed my hand tight and spoke to me through it – even though his voice was wobbly and he sighed whenever it broke mid-sentence. He got me to the other end.

We didn't really speak after that, not on the residential and hardly ever in school. It was only when he and Kennedy started doing something that could be seen as dating that I even acknowledged him, when I told Kennedy he was nice and genuine and if Kennedy really liked him, he should go for him.

Which was the primary reason I was so pissed off when Devon had screwed Kennedy over, because I was the reason Kennedy trusted him.

But right now, as I sat next to him, his eyes not leaving my face, that didn't matter because Kennedy had gotten over it; in fact, Kennedy had gotten Stephen from the whole ordeal and they were as happy as they could be.

I put my hand out to him.

His eyes dropped to my hand.

"I'll hold your hand if you hold mine, and I won't let go at any point," I told him. He swallowed. "I will get you out the other side."

He shook his head. "This is nothing like caving."

I nodded. "It is. It's dark, and neither of us want to do it."

"I do," he said forcefully.

"What are you doing next year, Devon?"

"Nothing. I'm…"

"Devon," I said softly.

His eyes met mine again. "I've got a place at the Institute of Music to study singing."

"You accepted?"

"Unconditional. It came through last week."

"You have so much to look forward to," I said then sighed when I remembered what he'd told me earlier. "Sorry, you said you wanted me not to speak to you like I'm the Queen, so I'm insanely jealous that you've got a place there, and I know you'll be amazing. You just need to live to *be* amazing." I pushed my hand a little closer.

He put his hand into mine. I squeezed them tight, standing up and pulling him up with me. He stumbled to his feet, taking a staggered step forward, and then he began to cry, his body shaking against mine, so I hugged him, holding him until he grew quiet.

He took a few breaths against me before pushing me back, not harshly, not at all, but enough that we were steps apart.

He took a few more deep breaths then he turned

from me and walked back towards the school, so I followed.

Finn was in the doorway again, still drinking from his mug but also scrolling through his phone. He looked up when we came through the door.

"Cassidy," he said, the confusion clear. "Didn't you *just* go to bed?"

"I can see why you thought that," I replied. He shook his head and laughed.

"I need your help," Devon said. "I... I almost did something and I need some help."

"Okay," Finn said as he slid his phone back into his pocket. "Let's... let's have a chat." He directed Devon down the opposite corridor to the boarding house.

Devon turned back to look at me just before they stepped through the door.

"Thank you," he said then swallowed deeply. "Thank you, Cassidy."

Sixteen

Kennedy didn't come back to the boarding house after the party. Instead, I found a text from him when I woke up telling me he was in Stephen's room, and asking me why we weren't speaking to Theo.

Cassidy: he's not who he says he is.

The King: What happened? The party ended once you left. It was quite incredible but Theo was pissed. What did he do?

I had basically typed it all out and then I stared at it, my thumb hovering over the send button before I erased it all.

Cassidy: I'll tell you later.
Cassidy: I'm going to Casper's. I need a

break.

The King: Stay safe.

Casper met me at the door of his boarding house. He looked thoroughly amused on the other side as he stepped back to let me in, then reached out his hand to me so I took it, letting him lead me down towards his room.

"I've been looking forward to this all week," he said softly as he swung our hands between us.

I frowned. "Why?"

"Were you just *never* going to tell me you had a famous father?" he asked. I rolled my eyes. "And that we could be front page news at any time."

I laughed. "I'm sorry about that, by the way."

He shook his head. "Don't be, it's possibly the coolest thing that's happened to me so far. I got a text from Cam, who'd had a call from Max because he recognised the back of my head; well, he thought it was Cam's and then he realised.

"Nick and I ran out on our break to buy a copy. It was awesome," he said in a laugh, so I smiled at him. "Everyone was pretty impressed. My entire class couldn't believe I'd been seen kissing a Raven. How dare I." He smiled at me as he unlocked a door.

The room was messy, messier than when we'd visited last week to pick up his trumpet. It was as if the other occupants of his room had dropped by, thrown everything in then left again, and I'd have believed that if Casper's bed wasn't also a mess. He laughed as he carefully stepped onto the bed, standing on it before crossing his legs and sitting down.

"I was making bracelets."

"You were what?" I said as I carefully sat opposite him. Between us was an open case with multiple pieces of thread.

"I was bored, so I decided to make some bracelets. It's pretty relaxing, so grab some thread and make one. You seem like you have a lot on your mind."

"A lot has happened since last week," I said as I pulled on the purple piece of thread.

"So… you came here to break up with me?"

"No," I answered quickly. He rose his head to meet my eyes. "No, I came here for a break from everything, because I wanted to see you, because this, you and me, is probably the most real thing about me right now."

"I like you, too," he told me.

I smiled as I pulled on the white thread. "I *am* sorry about the magazine. I know you think it's cool and all, but I am sorry. My father, he's not too impressed," I said, then looked down as I started to plait a yellow thread with the purple and white.

"He wants me to go on a date with an MP's son so he looks supportive, but also so who I'm fucking is notable."

"Oh," he said softly. I sighed. "I understand. I won't think you're cheating or…"

"I'm not going," I told him. We looked up together.

"I refuse to, because you're far more important to me."

"Cassidy, I appreciate that. Honestly, but this is your family."

"No," I said lightly. "Kennedy isn't asking me to do this, nor is my mum, *or* Harrison. They're my family."

"What's in it for him then?"

"The diversity vote, I guess. Showing people he isn't a homophobic bigot. Which he is."

"I'm sorry," he said, shaking his head. I shook mine back.

"You know he cut me off," I said. "He said that if I went on this date, he'd reinstate me."

"You should go on the date."

"No," I said in a laugh.

"But you should, Cassidy. I know we had fun last week, but you're…"

"You know what I'm most annoyed at?" I said. He shook his head, biting his lip. "I have a savings account. I've had a savings account since I was sixteen and I made my decision.

"My father gave us a grand a month. Kennedy and I both got a grand allowance since our sixteenth birthday. I saved five hundred pounds of it a month…"

"That's twelve hundred," he said.

I pointed at him. "*That's* impressive maths."

"Thanks, it's a skill."

"I mean, its twelve hundred give or take. Some months required spending more, some I spent less."

"Okay, so why are you telling me this? Except for invoking jealousy and making me wonder why we did

201

London on a budget last week?"

I thought he'd bring that up. He wasn't angry; he was smiling at me. "I don't use my savings account," I said, "*ever*. I haven't touched it since I opened it because I decided the moment I leave school, and I mean the *moment*, I was going to cut myself off from my family."

"*What?*" he whispered; I shook my head as I continued plaiting the thread.

"I just mean I was going to cut myself off from my father. Stop accepting his money, and just dissociate myself with his name.

"I had *no* idea he was going to run in the election. I could never have predicted that. I couldn't predict you either to be honest, but I had planned to move to London and just audition, audition and audition until I got somewhere.

"I'm pissed because he beat me to it. He cut me off before I got a chance to stand in front of him and tell him that I was walking away from him.

"Then, he offered to reinstate me if I went on this date, and I just... I..."

"Couldn't decide whether you say yes and continue collecting the money for three more months, or just stay cut off?"

"Yes," I said softly then shrugged. "Then I realised the decision was easy."

"Why?" he asked.

"Because of you. I figured it was time to stop doing what people expected of me and start doing what I want to. I want to be with you and I don't want to fuck it up by doing something for my father that you say is okay, but will probably resent later."

"I wouldn't…"

"I would," I said, then held up the bracelet to him. He frowned softly at me then held his hand out so I could tie the bracelet around his wrist.

"Cute," he said. "I'm not going to have sex with you."

"I gave you a bracelet, I didn't…"

"No, but I thought I best clear that up."

"What, ever?"

"Oh no," he said shaking his head. "I will at some point. I just…"

"I can wait," I said. "I'm happy to wait."

"Really?"

"Why?"

"You have a reputation, Cassidy," he told me. I laughed then covered my mouth. "I've done it once, literally. I'm not acting coy and pretending I'm an innocent snowflake. I've only done it once before."

"That's okay," I said shrugging. "It doesn't make much of a difference to me. I like you because I like *you*, not because I'm just after sex. My reputation obviously precedes me."

"I just, I worry about being disappointing. You're the Queen."

"I don't think it's even a possibility that you'd be disappointing."

"No?"

"No." I paused as I cleaned under my nail. "Besides,

I'm really good at telling someone what I want and getting it."

"What?" he said, his voice weak, so I looked up towards him then I shrugged.

"I'm just saying."

"We can make out," he said quickly then he laughed. "Wow I'm weak."

"I've never *just* made out," I told him, "but I am *all* for it."

"You've never just made out? It's one of the best things about being with someone."

I shrugged. "Why don't you prove that then?"

He leant forward, pausing briefly, his eyes searching around my face quickly so I kissed him.

Our lips barely touched before I lowered my head and he laughed, lifting my head so he could kiss me again.

We continued to make out until his phone began to vibrate against the bedside cabinet, the sound loud and repetitive. He sighed and picked it up.

"Who'd have a twin," he muttered, and I couldn't help but laugh, covering my mouth before hiding my face in his shoulder. "They're ordering pizza, do we want to join them?"

"Twins have uses sometimes."

He looked down at me, so I grinned and sat up, kissing him again.

"I guess I'll go freshen up," I said. He nodded, biting his lip. I took a moment to look at how ruined he looked, and took pleasure in the fact I'd done that. Until I looked at myself in the bathroom mirror and saw how ruined I also looked.

"Yeah, I did that," Casper said, nodding. I looked at him as he stood in the doorway, and my chest fluttered as his eyes prowled me

"Pizza," I said. He couldn't seem to take his eyes off me. My pulse was racing, my legs turning weak. "Casper."

"Yes," he said.

I took a step towards him, then another, until I was stood in front of him. He looked up at me, his head naturally moving towards me. I bit my lip.

"Pizza," I whispered.

"Yeah," he whispered back. I laughed.

"Hello," I whispered. He shook his head. "Are you back?"

"I am," he told me, and his cheeks flushed. I put my hand out to him. He smiled, taking my hand, and squeezed it before tugging on it and pulling me forward so he could step past me. He winked at me over his shoulder as he stood to the toilet. "Yes, our relationship has reached this point," he said before turning away from me. I laughed, leaning back against the sink.

"Oh, honey, I'd have been disappointed if we hadn't."

He laughed, shaking his head slowly before zipping up and turning to wash his hands. He took mine once he'd dried them, tugging on me so I followed him. We ran the corridor, passing door after door until we reached the end.

A plaque above the big grand double doors read *Auditorium.*

"Nick and Thomas got into so much trouble when we were in fifth year for doing this," he said as he got his card out his pocket and swiped us into the auditorium. "We have a rule that music students can't be on the theatre campus and vice versa. They'd been dating since they were like fourteen. Nick gave Thomas a card to our campus so they could spend time together."

"They were caught?"

"They were caught," he confirmed, sounding delighted. "It was *massive*. Nick had never gotten into trouble before or anything. It was scandalous."

"Did the rules change?"

"Kind of. As we're last years they don't really care anymore, and I've always been able to go between the two because of Cam. Sometimes I just snuck Nick in with me because my card wouldn't set off any alarms," he said as he touched his card to the identical door that we'd walked towards.

It clicked open, and he looked smug.

The musical theatre side of the campus wasn't all that different to the music side, the carpets as plush as the walls were bare, except for the alumni photos that were right near to the door.

I couldn't help but look at them. Finding the picture from just two years ago with the boy, Xander, who'd been our waiter.

"Graduating class," Casper said from behind me, "will be our turn this year."

I smiled as my eyes jumped over class after class all the way back through the nineties, through the eighties.

"No way," I whispered, taking a step closer. Casper also did.

"What?"

"Finn," I said, then turned to look at Casper as he shook his head. "He's our theatre director. He's my mentor."

"Traitor," Casper said in a gasp.

"He's done worse things, I can assure you," I laughed. He took my hand, weaving me through the corridors towards a hall with two doors.

He knocked with both hands continuously until it opened.

"God, we heard you," Zack exclaimed as he held the door before swinging it shut again.

"You're an asshole," Casper declared. I laughed behind him, covering my mouth as the door opened again to Zack, stood with his hand over his chest.

"Ow."

"Let us in," Casper said. Zack scrunched his nose, examining us both.

"I'll let the Queen in."

Casper tutted, turning to look at me, his expression softening.

"I like that I'm also the Queen *here*," I told him. "I feel like the universe is in balance."

He laughed, then pushed my shoulder, so I pulled my tongue back at him.

It was late when I got back to the boarding house. I nodded to my English teacher who was on night patrol, smiling pleasantly at her and wishing her a goodnight before walking down to my room.

My corridor was quiet, but I hadn't expected anything else on a Sunday evening. I pushed open the door with my shoulder, looking towards Kennedy's bed and frowning slightly as he and Cody looked back at me.

"What?" I said quietly. Kennedy stood from his bed. He looked like he was going to try and calm me, ensure I didn't lose my head.

Then I saw Theo and understood why. I knew I was definitely going to lose my *fucking* head.

"Get out." I pushed the door open further. Theo stood from his bed quicker than I'd ever seen before. "You are not welcome here. Get out."

"Fuck you," Theo hissed at me. I threw my jacket onto my bed, walking towards him. Kennedy grabbed me before I threw myself at him.

"Calm down, Cassidy, hear him out," he said.

Adrenaline shot through my body, my hands shaking. "Hear him out? Are you for real? He's been spreading my secrets around the whole fucking school. He's been manipulating Devon; he's probably been manipulating so many other people.

"How did you find out about Finn? Huh? It wasn't because I told Devon, because he wasn't doing anything with that, you were who fuelled it. You made him blackmail me. How did you find out about Finn?"

"I saw you," he spat back.

208

I shook my head. "We were careful."

"No, you *fucking* weren't, you were dripping. Every time you were near each other you might as well have stripped and fucked right in front of us.

"You were *not* discreet, ever. Everyone else is just turning a blind eye to you, because of course the slut Cassidy is being fucked by the theatre teacher."

"Fuck you," I shouted at him; Kennedy grabbed me tighter.

"What did you think it was? Love? Did you think Finn loved you? Because he *didn't*. He was just getting his rocks off and you were an easy fuck." He laughed; it was sly. "I saw you two kissing backstage. You didn't even try to hide it. I thought it was nothing, then Devon confirmed it."

"You almost killed him," I growled at him. "Didn't you even realise what you were doing?"

"He doesn't matter," he spat back at me, "he was just there to—"

Cody punched him.

"Cody!" Kennedy gasped as Cody shook his hand.

"Fuck you, Theo. How dare you stand there and say he doesn't matter."

Theo pushed him; Cody didn't even stumble.

"Just because you want to be fucking Cassidy, too."

"Oh, sweetheart, I think it's you who wants to be doing that," Cody said as he walked towards him, "because I don't need to wonder what that's like."

"Why would I want *that*?" Theo hissed.

Cody laughed. "Because you've never had the chance,

have you? Couldn't handle the fact he had Finn either, could you?"

"But of course, he didn't even have the balls to threaten me himself," I said. Theo looked at me. "Using Devon, because, what? He was an easy target? After all that shit, he was an easy target?"

"Proved how much of a slut you are," Theo snarled. "It was *his* idea to send you the notes. *His* idea to make you think you'd be stood up, *his* idea to meet you at the theatre. You, the *slut* that you are, couldn't resist."

"How long have you hated me?" I asked. He looked straight at me. "*Well* go on, how long?"

"Always."

I sat up long after Kennedy and Cody had fallen asleep. Theo was gone. He hadn't stood a chance and I'd barely told him to get out again before Kennedy physically got him out. I had thought about calling Casper, but it was well after curfew had passed and I figured he'd likely be asleep. I didn't want to wake him.

Nor did I want him to worry when he woke up before me and saw my texts. I thought about leaving the room myself, walking the woods, smoking some weed and forgetting about everything, but that didn't happen either.

Instead, I sat at the head of my bed, my face buried deep into my knees, and I sobbed. I fucking sobbed and I hated myself for it.

I hated Theo for it for making me feel this way, but also because I let him.

I don't know how long I'd been sat that way; I didn't know what time it was or if the day had broken, so I couldn't be blamed when I jumped violently at arms wrapping around me.

"It's okay," Kennedy whispered into my ear; I shook my head. "No, no it's okay that he made you cry."

Damn him for knowing me so well.

"No it's not," I gasped.

He hugged me a little tighter. "It is, Cassidy."

I looked up and towards him. He pushed my hair back out of my face.

"I shouldn't let him have this power over me, I shouldn't."

"He hurt you," he whispered. "He *knows* you and he used it to hurt you. Cassidy, you're allowed to cry after something like that."

"He thinks those things about me." I swallowed. "*Everyone* thinks those things about me."

"No."

"*Yes.*" I swallowed, shaking my head. "*Yes,* I am just the slut who is easy to get into bed and won't say no to anyone. I'm just the person who no one really likes but they tolerate. Who is going along blissfully unaware of all the hate and whispers behind my back."

"That's not true and you know it."

"Do I?" He met my eyes. "Do I, Kennedy? Because, thinking about it, *really* thinking about it, who's my best friend? Who's even just my friend here?"

"Cody," he answered.

I laughed, turning to face Cody's bed. "*Your* best

friend," I replied. "Your best friend likes me. Yay."

"Archie."

"He's fourteen. I love him, I do, but he's fourteen. He's a baby, Kennedy."

"Finn," he whispered; I held my breath.

"I didn't realise..." I sighed. "I didn't... he's right because I didn't realise until I met Casper's friends that *no one* here liked me."

"What do you mean?" he whispered.

My voice quivered before I settled myself. "They hardly knew me. They knew that Casper liked me and they knew I was the Queen, but that was it and they were kind. They were kind to me and spoke to me, laughed with me.

"They didn't try anything on with me, nor did we need excessive alcohol, or weed or whatever. They were there, interested in me. Before I came back today, I was with them. We had pizza in their room and we talked and laughed. We sang and we played stupid little games that meant the world to me.

"They're my friends, Kennedy. These boys who I've known for what, two weeks? They're my friends and all the people here, they mean nothing to me, and I mean nothing to them."

"That isn't true."

"Yes, it is," I murmured. "*Yes, it is.* He was right about all of that, he was right about everything."

"Not everything," he whispered directly into my ear. "You're not a slut," he said, "*at all.* You're not a slut. Do you know why I know that?"

"Because you're trying to make me feel better?"

"No," he laughed. "No, because of Casper."

"I haven't liked anyone as much as I like Casper."

"I know that, too."

"I think I'm genderqueer."

"I didn't know that," he said.

I looked up at him as I wiped my face. "Actually, I don't think, I *know* I am. Casper has been helping me figure that out and I guess I fell in love with him by accident."

"By accident?" Kennedy repeated. I shrugged lightly. He kissed my cheek. "Theo's wrong. You're just loving and caring and, well, I guess you like sex and there's nothing wrong with that, but how dedicated you are to Casper, how, I guess, faithful you are to that relationship shows you're not a slut."

I wasn't ready to believe him. He sighed, leaning his forehead against mine.

"I'm sorry I woke you up."

"Don't you dare," he whispered. I looked at him as he cuddled me a little closer. "Don't apologise for that. Ever. You can wake me up whenever you need to, even if we're not in the same room. Got it?"

"Got it," I replied, then, "same for you, you know."

"Oh, I know. Don't you worry, you'll be woken up in the dead of night for many years to come, Queen."

"Thank you, your Majesty," I whispered then, "can you stay…"

"I planned to," he said, nodding. "It wasn't even a consideration that I was getting out of this bed." He tugged on my quilt so he could get underneath it. "Do you know at which point we got too big to do this?" he whispered as I lay facing him. We were too big for my single bed, that was true, but I definitely didn't know when that had happened. It felt like it was only recently we'd stopped sneaking into each other's beds of a night, when in reality it had been five years since we'd last slept like this.

Five whole years.

Seventeen

I hid in the theatre.

I skipped classes for the day and I slept in, then I went to hide in the theatre. Finn wasn't there; I didn't know exactly where he was, although I figured he was probably teaching. It was quiet, and dark.

I walked up towards the lighting desk, turning on the little desk lamp before stroking my fingers over the sliders on the sound desk, before pressing the buttons for the lights.

I watched as the stage came to life, smiling briefly before pulling down the white light and making it look far softer, pushing up the red and the blue until a purple haze fell over the stage.

I walked through the dark stalls, walked up the stairs and stood in the middle of the stage.

I took a deep breath and then I began to sing, because if my life were a musical it'd be time for my eleven o'clock number. When the main character stands centre stage with just a spotlight and sings about their feelings. It'd be my 'She Used to be Mine', or 'I Dreamed a Dream'.

It was my moment to fall apart and be put back together again by the end of the chorus, to then go and get the biggest ass cheer the audience could muster before the joyous finale.

It worked, mostly, and I wasn't surprised when an applause came from the back of the theatre. I was even less surprised when I saw it was Finn.

I sat myself on the edge of the stage.

"Skipping classes, huh?" he said as he walked down the stalls.

I shrugged. "Needed a mental health day," I replied without looking up at him. We didn't speak again until he sat down beside me. He went to wrap his arms around me. I flinched away, pretending I didn't see the hurt on his face.

"Cassidy."

"We can't be together like this. What if we get caught, what if…?"

"Fuck it," he whispered, then wrapped his arms around me, squeezing me tightly. I swallowed against him, trying to repress the tears that were threatening again, but I wasn't going to let them out because I'd already done my damn ballad. "You need a hug, Cassidy. I'm going to give you one."

I hugged him back tighter as I breathed him in.

"I've missed you," I told him. He sighed against me. "So much. I don't mean the sex, even though yeah, I kind of miss that. I mean…"

"The talking," he whispered. I nodded as I moved back from the hug.

"I can't talk to anyone else," I said in a quiet voice. "No one, because Kennedy has Stephen, and sure there's Casper but we're in the early days of this relationship and I don't wish to scare him off."

"I am still your mentor," he said.

I shook my head. "You said…"

"Yes, whilst we tried to figure things out, and well… we figured things out."

"Did we?" I asked.

He nodded. "Devon's going to be okay. He's not in the best place, granted, but he will be okay. He's gone home. He's taking some time off."

"Will he still graduate?" I asked.

He nodded slowly as he kicked his legs. "Yes." He looked straight at me. I frowned back. "We'd never fail someone for poor mental health. *Never.*"

"Preston really impacted this school in a good way, didn't he?"

"This and others."

"So, because Devon's not here we can sit next to each other?"

"No, but he apologised," he said. I didn't understand. "That night, when we were talking, he just told me he was sorry and he shouldn't have threatened us. I forgave him, but Cassidy, I should *not* have had sex with you, even once. Never mind as many times as I did."

"I know it was wrong," I said. He looked down. "I

know it shouldn't have happened and I know we totally risked your job, your entire life, but I didn't help. I wanted to sleep with you, I wanted to be with you, and I enjoyed it every single time. It's not all your fault."

"But it's an abuse of my power."

"No," I said softly. "No, I mean *yes* usually this situation is totally an abuse of power and a whole lot of bad, but Finn, I love you and *yes* I mean that romantically, but I also mean it as you're my best friend."

He almost looked as if he felt sorry for me.

"When I leave here, there's only two people I want to make sure I stay in contact with, and that's Archie, because that boy should rule someday, and *you*.

"I want to be your friend. I want to text you stupid memes and get excited over theatre news with you. Send you a message telling you I've booked tickets to see *Les Mis* and you're coming with me if you like, or not.

"I want you to rant to me when it comes to the winter showcase and the summer musical. I want you to tell me about your day and send me your ideas, even the terrible ones. I want us to be friends."

"I want us to be friends, too," he replied.

I smiled then rose my eyebrow at him. "But we need to talk about you being a Golden boy."

He laughed loudly, a quick bark of a sound as he hit the stage. "How did you find that out?"

"I saw your alumni photograph."

He frowned.

"I was in my boyfriend's dorm," I added.

"Graduated almost ten years ago now. I loved every

minute of that school."

"Why didn't you teach there?" I asked.

"For real? The teachers in that school are phenomenal. I'm just good I guess; I teach Drama, I don't teach Performing Arts."

"You're better than you think," I told him.

He shrugged lightly. "I love this job, and as much as I loved that school, I think I enjoy that this school isn't purely musical theatre, that this school has other things going on and only those who love it join the theatre. I graduated, did my teaching degree and, well, I couldn't leave once I did my placement here, could I?"

"Why not?"

"Well..." he said quietly. "There was this little eleven-year-old who I was allocated as a mentor to. He was brassy, had a hell of an unbroken voice on him but he was also really shy and used to..." His eyes roamed me. "And still hides behind a faux confidence, a persona. I couldn't leave him."

"Thank you," I whispered, resting my head on his shoulder and squeezing my eyes shut.

"I know it feels like the end of the world right now, but the people you know in school? The people you roomed with, the people you sleep with. They don't usually come into the real world with you.

"You're friends because of circumstance. Soon, you'll make friends because they have the same interests as you."

"You know what happened with Theo?"

"Archie told me," he said softly. I frowned. "I was

with his class before I came here. I set work, and he appeared at my side and updated me on everything. Impressively whilst doing the work."

"Archie is impressive like that," I agreed. "What exactly did he tell you?"

"He told me a lot of what Devon had, how it was Theo who'd been causing all the trouble, and that you'd found out. You kicked him out of your room?"

"Twice," I said, nodding. "He said no one here likes me, that he's always hated me."

"Because they're all jealous of you," he said. I rolled my eyes. "Cassidy, you're the *Queen*."

"A self-proclaimed title."

"Do you *really* think if the majority of this school didn't kiss the ground you walked on, they'd refer to you as the Queen? It wouldn't have lasted a week, Cassidy."

"It lasted because of Kennedy."

"And who made Kennedy?"

I looked at him. He rose an eyebrow at me.

"I've known you for seven years, Cassidy, and I mean *known*. I love Kennedy, fully respect him but, honey, he wouldn't have gotten anywhere without you."

"That's true," I murmured; he leaned into my shoulder.

"I can kick Theo out of theatre?" he whispered to me.

I smiled at him, already knowing the answer to that. "No. I am the Queen. It'll kill him to see me not caring."

"Exactly," he whispered, then looked down between us as my phone vibrated against the stage. I rose an eyebrow at him as I pulled it out of my pocket.

Not Cameron: Heard you're skipping. Can I skip with you?

      Cassidy: Wouldn't want to be a bad influence on you.

Not Cameron: Too late. I've got something I want to show you. Let's meet for lunch.

I glanced up at Finn from my phone.

"Do you feel better?"

"Significantly," I said, nodding. "I still think I'm going to skip the entire day though."

"Take the mental health day. All of it. I'll see you tomorrow."

I nodded.

"For our rehearsal," I said as I stood from the stage, "in which I *am* the Squib," I said dramatically. He laughed happily, applauding me as I left the stage.

Casper was stood outside the coffee shop we were meeting at, still in his uniform, scrolling through his phone. He looked up when he heard me approach. He lifted his finger almost instantly to me.

"Don't say anything."

"I like your…"

"Shush," he replied as I walked closer to him.

"But your *tie* is…"

"Quiet," he said, laughing as I stepped close enough he could put his finger on my lips. "I had to leave school in my uniform so they thought I was just leaving for lunch. I'm going to get changed," he told me, then took his finger away.

I smirked. "You look so cute."

"Shut up," he said, laughing. I pulled him towards me, smiling at him before kissing him lightly. "Come on," he whispered, taking my hand and walking me into the coffee shop. He sat me at a table, smirking at me before he walked away into the bathroom to change.

He placed a coffee down in front of me when he returned.

"*Oh*, now you're kind of hot," I said. He winked. "How did you know I was skipping?" I asked as I lifted my coffee. The smell of it brought a smile to my face.

"Your brother sent me a text," he said. I frowned at him.

"*Excuse me?*"

"Hey Casper, this is Kennedy. Got your number from Cass's phone. Benefits of having the same face, winky face." He looked up at me, raising his eyebrow at me. "He's having a pretty bad day, skipping classes, thought you might be able to help."

"I think he meant like a nice text, not you skipping with me."

"I can put my uniform back on and go back to Maths, if you want?"

"No," I whispered. He grinned as I got my phone out of my pocket. "That sneak," I muttered as I looked through my past phone unlocks.

"Got to get yourself a new face," he said simply. I laughed. "What's wrong, what's happened?"

"I don't want to go through this again," I moaned. He looked up and grinned charmingly at the waitress as she placed two sandwiches down in front of us.

"Is it your dad stuff?"

"No," I replied, hearing the inclination in my voice, "that's not even the cherry on top." I rubbed my forehead. "What did you want to show me?"

"Let's have lunch first," he offered. I nodded, lifting the top layer of bread from the sandwich. "There's no tomato," he said as he picked up his own. We looked up at the same time. He winked at me.

"I kind of *really* like you, you know."

"I know," he said softly. I tilted my head at him. "Because I kind of really like you too."

We got the Tube towards wherever it was he was taking me. The train was so empty that we could've sat on opposite ends of the carriage, but instead we sat *right* next to each other.

He walked me down a street of pink, yellow, baby blue and pale green houses, Most of them had flowers on their windowsills. I stopped to look at them.

"Where are we?" I asked, turning on the spot until I saw Casper. He was smiling back at me.

"Home," he answered.

I frowned. "You lived in Blackpool."

He nodded, holding his hand out to me, so I walked

223

towards him, squeezing his hand when I took hold of it.

"Cameron is moving in with Max," he said. I had no idea where this was going. He pulled me a little closer to him. "Nick and Thomas are going to New York for a fortnight before coming back and looking for somewhere to live together."

"Right?" I said slowly. He smiled at me.

"Harley and I got talking about all this. We decided living together was a pretty good idea."

"That *is* a good idea."

He held up a key between us.

"So when you say home, you mean…"

"This is going to be my home," he confirmed, grinning and walking away from me towards the front door of the pale green house. He unlocked the door, pushed it open and stepped into the hallway. I followed. "We figured Nick and Thomas could live here whilst they're looking for their own place. Zack could stay if he wanted to, there's four bedrooms, so it'd just make sense." He continued as he walked further into the house. I closed the front door behind us.

"Why did you want to show me?" I asked as I followed him into the living room.

"Wait, really?" he asked. I shrugged. "Cassidy, I was thinking about what you said yesterday about cutting yourself off from your father." He smiled. "I was going to ask you to move in with us."

"Isn't that a bit quick?"

"To be roommates? No, I don't think so."

I laughed as he smiled at me.

"We can sleep in different rooms if you want, there are four."

"I…" I laughed. "I don't think that'll be necessary."

"Good."

"You've bought this place, like it's official?"

"We've put a deposit down," he said, nodding as he started up the stairs, so I followed. "Got the keys, can move in when we graduate. We're paying rent until we do of course."

We walked into a bedroom.

"This is the room I've dibbed," he said as he sat on the bare bed. "Up to your standard?"

I walked towards him, standing between his legs and lifting his chin. He rose his eyebrow at me. I kissed him, feeling him laugh against me, his hands resting on the back of my head as he deepened the kiss.

He lowered his head, resting his forehead against my nose, then laughed.

"I'll take that as a yes."

"You should definitely take that as a yes."

He kissed me again.

"Is Harley happy with this?"

"With the house?" he asked. I shook my head, pointing between us. "Oh, yeah, he likes you and he really likes me. He can't wait and has really good headphones."

"Good," I whispered then kissed him again. His ears turned pink as I moved closer to whisper into them. "I like to sing really loud."

He coughed, the pink spreading to his cheeks. I

pulled my tongue at him. He tried to catch it back in a kiss.

"I can see a nice peppermint on these walls," I whispered, and I was sure he could feel my lips moving against his. It was confirmed when he sighed. "A feature wall too, stripped I think."

"Stop talking," he whispered, pulling me over himself onto the bed, kneeling above me and putting his hand over my mouth. "You can have full decoration privileges, I promise." He moved his hand to kiss me. He didn't move too far back. "Peppermint, really?"

"Yes. We can raise a cactus," I added. He laughed happily.

"Theo sounds like the worst kind of dick," Casper said as we sat on the wood decking in the small garden of the house. There wasn't much grass at all, just concrete and a few empty flowerpots. I was smoking because I'd started telling him what had conspired and got worked up. So we'd chosen to sit outside. He'd commented that smoking was a bad habit again. I told him to fuck off.

"So, he's been your friend since the beginning?"

"Basically…" I said, nodding.

I had arrived with Kennedy, of course. We were put in our room and there was not even a consideration we wouldn't be roomed together. The school only separated twins if it was requested. Cody came later that evening after we'd gone for tea. He was just in our room looking a bit lost. Theo arrived before Cody could tell us apart.

They spent the first night trying to figure out which

of us was Kennedy and which of us was Cassidy. They hadn't figured it out before we went to bed, but they started to.

I went to the theatre audition with Theo the next day. We'd whispered and planned for it the entire day; after that Theo knew that I was Cassidy and we got closer.

He was my first kiss with a boy when we were thirteen, because I knew I was gay. I was *definitely* sure I was gay. He wasn't too sure, so we had kissed.

He was the first person I drank vodka with when we were fourteen and definitely shouldn't have been sharing the bottle in Rowan's back garden.

He was the first shopping spree on Oxford Street.

He was the first cigarette when we were sixteen and we shared one, again, in Rowan's back garden.

He was so many of my firsts, and I trusted him. I trusted him so much.

But I hadn't trusted him with Finn, I hadn't trusted him when Kennedy whispered to me about Stephen. I hadn't trusted him about Casper, and I don't know if that was because I had an inkling – even though that might be giving myself too much credit, because I had no clue.

"It's okay that you had no idea, you know," he said softly.

I sighed. "No, it's not. I should've been at least aware."

"Why?"

"I'm the Queen."

"Yeah, I can name multiple Queens who got assassinated."

227

"Thanks, Casper," I said.

He laughed. "My point is that you usually don't know the betrayer until it's too late."

"Right," I said in a breath. "You're right."

"What are you going to do now? There's two months left of school."

"I'm going to walk into that theatre, into every single rehearsal, and act like he doesn't exist," I stated, "but I'm probably going to skip any parties."

"Why?" he asked. I shrugged lightly. "You like parties, right? You enjoy going to parties. Why stop because he's there?"

"It's not because *he's* there. It's just, I used to go to parties to have sex, not much else. I'd rather spend an evening with... you."

"Ah," he said.

I cringed. "I don't mean having sex, oh my god." I moaned, resting my head into my hands. "I'm not obsessed, I swear."

"It's okay," he said softly. "I think we need to talk about it. Sex is a bit complicated, for me." He closed his eyes, shaking his head. "I trust you, right. We're going to live together; this is really embarrassing."

"If you can't talk about the embarrassing parts of sex with me, we shouldn't be doing it yet."

He met my eyes. I shrugged.

"I fully believe that. If we can't talk about the messy bits, it's not right yet. It's why when I started having sex, I'd only sleep with the boys who didn't giggle when I said the word condom."

"I don't giggle at condom," he said. I nodded. "It's just... It takes a really long time for me to be comfortable with the idea of sex, right?"

"Right," I said slowly.

"I don't know what it is. I don't know if it's issues with my body."

"Dysphoria?" I asked. I could tell he felt uncomfortable talking about this.

"I'm quite content a lot of the time. Dysphoria is a quiet buzz in the back of my mind but when I feel fem it's a bit encompassing. Sex is a no-go. I don't even touch myself those days. I can't because I don't want a dick."

"I get that," I said. He shook his head. "I honestly get that, but I want you to understand that if *ever* you don't want to have sex with me, or you feel uncomfortable and you tell me to stop, I will, or if you say no, we won't do *any*thing."

"I..." He took a staggered breath out. "Thank you."

"And I mean even if we've already fooled around, you can still say no."

He paused, looking confused

"What?"

"Don't you count fooling around as sex?"

"It's a type of sex..." I said slowly. "But things like blowjobs and hand jobs, they're fun, they're foreplay and... why?"

"I've..." he began, then blushed brightly, looking away from me.

"Never done that?"

"No," he whispered, then cleared his throat, turning

to me fully. "I slept with Harley," he said. I rose my eyebrow at him. He waved his hands at me. "We've always flirted, always, but Cam's his best friend and it was just, weird. Anyway, we slept together because we trusted each other and everyone else had lost their virginities, and you know, I didn't want to leave school without it. It's stupid in hindsight. I didn't know you were in my future but whatever. I love Harley and it was okay, but we just had sex, we didn't fool around."

"So you've never?"

"No," he said softly, "never. I've never, not even at parties. I'm so lame."

"No," I repeated, smiling at him as I squeezed his knee, "not lame. No way."

"Really?"

"Really," I assured him. "I know you're probably thinking I'm just trying to make you feel better, but I have sex for fun. I can't say I've ever had sex for love. Some people don't have sex for fun, just for love, and that is okay.

"I don't judge how anyone has sex. It's personal preference, it's a personal experience."

"You still manage to surprise me," he muttered.

"I'm going to be doing that for a long time," I told him. He laughed, knocking his head against mine, then kissed me.

"I've been putting off everything with you because I count it all as sex."

"That's okay," I said. He covered my mouth, shushing me, so I laughed.

"No. No, because I *want* to do these things with you, I'm just making excuses not to, for no reason."

"If you're not ready," I said after wrestling his hand off me. He tried to push my hand back.

"That's the thing though," he whispered. "I am. I have been; I wouldn't have slept with Harley otherwise. I wouldn't have been so eager, I guess, to do it if I wasn't ready," he sighed. "I... I'm sorry."

"No, no don't apologise," I said.

He sighed. "I *am* sorry. You've found yourself the most insecure person you could've. I've been lying to myself for years and pretending, hiding parts of myself. Out of fear I guess, out of loathing."

"Like what you said when we started this? You'd only just figured out..."

"Yeah. Cam came out without a problem to us; he's only just told our parents and I kind of figured I can't like boys too. Like I just can't, so I won't. I missed out on so many things because I refused to acknowledge the side of me that liked boys, and that is a huge part of me. Huge.

"I've only ever kissed Zack, and that was because Nick practically forced us together at a party when we were like fifteen. Harley and I barely kissed but I slept with him, and now you.

"I don't want to fuck this up with you because of my own insecurities, my own prejudice."

"Can I say...." I said slowly. He frowned at me lightly. "I would never have figured out I was genderqueer without you."

"Wait," he whispered. I smiled at him as he grinned

231

at me. "You figured out your word."

"I figured out my word," I agreed, "and I feel free. I didn't even know I was searching for a word, and then I found it. I don't think we have to be labelled. If you want to have a relationship with me and not have to tell anyone your sexuality, I'm fine with that, happy with that. Our relationship, our business, but even saying that you don't need to figure out your word if you don't want to."

"Thank you," he said with a frown, then he shook his head. "I want to have sex with you," he added. I bit my lip so I wouldn't smile too wide. "So bad, and I think I was extremely worried about sex ruining our relationship, or messing up this feeling, because this feeling is amazing.

"Sitting here with you, feeling relaxed and happy and, like, this is so right. Being able to say anything and not be embarrassed, being able to mess around and laugh and play. Doing anything and not feel like you'll laugh at me or use it against me at some point."

"I guess that's what a relationship is supposed to feel like," I said.

"I've never had that before."

"Neither have I," I told him, then lifted my hand, holding my little finger to him. He frowned but linked our pinkies together. "I promise sex won't make this any less comfortable," I said. He nodded, his finger wrapping tighter around mine. "I promise I won't let it and I promise to talk to you about anything that makes this any less comfortable. I promise to work through this with you and make sure we're doing this right."

CAMERON JAMES

He nodded, shaking our hands together before pulling me closer to him. He smiled at me so I smiled back, letting him kiss me, not breaking our hands as he did.

"I know you're going through a load of stuff right now," he said without moving away from me. I rose my eyes to look at him even though he kept his low, looking at our hands. "I know it's shit and you're not in the best place but, if you wanted to, we could."

I smiled. He looked up quickly.

"Have some sex," he added. I almost barked with my laugh, covering my mouth with my other hand as he also began to laugh.

"Here?" I asked, once my laughter had died down. He looked up towards the house then shrugged very lightly.

"I mean, this is I'm sure where we're going to be having sex for years to come. Why not start now?"

"You're the best."

He laughed happily as I broke our hands, resting my hand on his chin and kissing him deeply.

"What are we?"

"Don't worry, I've got you..." I whispered. He shivered under my hands so I smirked. "But if you don't want me to do anything at any point, tell me."

"I promise," he whispered. I winked at him then pushed him up by the chest.

"Stand," I requested. He frowned at me. "Stand up, stand up."

He stood, looking down at me, amused, until I knelt

233

in front of him and his mouth became a perfect 'o'.

"You're going to?"

"Yuh-huh," I said.

He nodded breathlessly. "How?"

"Well, I could sit here and tell you all about how I learnt to give blowjobs *or* I could suck your dick."

"I'm actually very interested in learning how you learnt," he said, a quirk in his voice, so I moved closer to him, stroking my thumb delicately over his crotch.

"Well..." I said softly. "I was tired of poor blowjobs," I told him as I continued to stroke him gently, "so I thought, why not learn how to do a good one." I reached for his button, not undoing it just yet. "I watched a *lot* of porn," I told him as I flicked open his button. He moaned then gasped, covering his mouth as I looked up at him. "Read a few articles. Did my research, you know." I tugged on his jeans. They gave quite easily, falling down his hips.

"I am going to side-track from my story to tell you that I *adore* your boxers," I said. He laughed, resting his head against the wall, shaking his head at me as I stroked my thumb near to his dick again. "Like orange and giraffes. I'm sold."

He laughed again, smiling down at me, his entire body finally relaxed. I smirked up at him as he chewed on his lip.

"So, I got a bit of practice in," I continued, slipping my thumbs under his boxer band. He watched me with interest as I lowered his waistband below his dick. "Soon I was able to..." I whispered, then, "do this."

I swallowed him down in one. More of a parlour trick than anything else, more to show off, but given the noise that came out his mouth, it was totally worth it.

Eighteen

The whispers had already started.

The King is leaving in a week, a new King must be chosen.

Names of boys flying around, trying to figure out their eligibility for the crown. Kennedy wasn't letting anything slip. He was tight-lipped and hiding himself with the football team so he wouldn't be asked any questions.

I was hiding myself in the theatre to avoid my own questions. Our show was far more important, it being a matter of hours away. We'd gotten through our tech rehearsal, our dress rehearsal, even our sitzprobe when the orchestra had come and played for us for the first time.

All was going well and, sure, occasionally I'd been unnecessarily rough in certain scenes with Theo, but now the stage was set, and it was almost time for opening night.

I had my highlighted book next to me on the stage, my microphone already fitted to my face, and I was breathing.

"Okay?" Finn said warily.

I opened my eyes as he walked towards me. "This is my last show," I told him. I looked him up and down. He wore the grey t-shirt with the *Be More Chill* logo on the breast that we'd all got three or so weeks ago when rehearsals got more intense. His had *Finn* on the back, *Director* underneath it.

The one I was wearing had *The Queen*, and *Squib* printed on it.

"How do you feel about that?"

"Scared," I answered. "Honestly? Terrified. Three days and this show is over. Two days later and school is over. What? Two weeks after that and I've graduated. Just like that, it's all done."

"And then you get to start your whole life, and we can go out for a drink without anyone caring."

"Plus point," I agreed. "I'm so scared. I'm moving in with Casper this weekend. That's pretty grown up. Kennedy and Stephen are off to Amsterdam after graduation. My father could become the prime minister next *fucking* Thursday."

"Okay," Finn said softly, "okay, let's get through Opening Night? Okay? Focus on one thing at a time. Get through the show tonight."

"The Golden Boys are in the audience tonight," I whispered. "Their show starts tomorrow; I'm going to see them on Friday and they are all coming to see me tonight."

"You're going to be sensational. You know that, right? You've been off book for weeks, you've been amazing, you know your blocking, your songs. Everything."

I nodded as I took a deep breath.

"I believe that you can do this. I fully believe you can do this."

"Drink. Next Saturday, after the election? Okay?"

"It's a deal," he confirmed then smiled at me. "No go backs."

I blew him a kiss. He caught it, winking at me, then nodding behind me.

I turned.

"What?" I snapped as Theo walked down stage. He sighed, holding his hands up to me.

"I want to talk to you."

"I *don't* want to talk to you," I snapped.

"Cassidy," Finn said softly. I closed my eyes.

"Let's talk," Theo offered. I sighed as I stood, picking up my book and walking towards him. I had nothing to say to him.

He was also wearing his grey t-shirt, *Theo* and *Michael* printed on the back, his microphone also fitted.

"We graduate in a week," he said. "It's been two months and I think we should try and fix this."

"This can't be fixed," I said, pointing between us. "I can't find any way to forgive you for everything."

"Hear me out," he said.

I nodded once. "Ten minutes. I'm going to give you

ten minutes."

He was jealous. Which is the whole top and bottom of it. It hadn't started that way of course. We were friends in first and second year. He was smug that he knew I was Cassidy. We shared secrets; we were best friends. I was ecstatic I had a friend that was mine. A friend that didn't refer to me as 'and Cassidy', or group me as 'the twins'. A friend that belonged one hundred percent to me.

Sure, he liked Kennedy. They were friends, but they weren't friends like Theo and I were.

It started towards the end of third year when King Asher's reign was coming to an end and there were whispers around the entire school, much like now, of everyone trying to figure out who the new King would be.

I liked Asher. A lot. I idolised him, his confidence and charisma. He was everything I wanted to be. Outspoken, revered, loved and so inexplicably proud. He didn't answer to anyone.

I followed him around like Archie followed me. I talked Kennedy up to him so much. He told me once before he left that if he could let me be King, he would.

I told him I'd rule like a Queen.

Theo didn't find it fair. Why did we get the popularity? Why did *we* become the King, become the Queen? Why did it all happen to me?

"It's not like you didn't get the benefits of it," I said.

He sighed, rubbing his forehead. "I didn't want to be popular. I wanted to do theatre, and just exist. I didn't want a thousand eyes on me every day, but you relished in it."

"It's an act," I told him. "It's always been an act. I liked Asher. I didn't start that friendship with popularity in mind. When I was thirteen, I wasn't thinking 'I'll rule this school one day'. I was just thinking 'look at this person who's so strong and proud'. Asher was queer and in power. Everyone loved him; everyone listened to him and invited him places.

"My father hated me," I stated. "From the moment I started showing flamboyant tendencies. The first time I sang a showtune or bought something covered in glitter. The first time my *fucking* wrist was limp. That man has hated me. He's wished me straight. He's wished me something different than I am.

"Asher showed me that I could be me without anyone caring. Asher, Finn, they both taught me to be myself, without giving a fuck about the consequences.

"I just so happened to become popular, become the Queen, because I started being myself. You want me to apologise for that? For being *myself?*"

"No," he said quietly. "I just… I didn't think it was fair." He sighed. "It was stupid, okay?"

"Please, tell me more," I mocked.

He sighed. "Devon was a stupid idea."

"You…"

"I know I was shitty to him. I know I almost destroyed him. Cody made it abundantly clear, believe me, but it was so simple. Especially after what he did to Kennedy. Which, by the way, was off his own back. Him and his gaggle of choir boys. They made that bet on their own, then we began to talk.

"He got information off me to take Kennedy down. Mostly about your father because Devon wanted to be popular, and I figured if he knocked Kennedy off the throne, you'd fall too and we'd fall under the radar."

"But Kennedy practically thrived from it."

"Literally," he said, sounding mildly frustrated. "So then we turned our attention to you, but I wasn't listening to him. He kept telling me how bad it was with the choir, how they'd fallen from grace, how there was no point. I just didn't listen."

"So, all you wanted was to fall off the radar?"

"Basically."

"Why didn't you just tell me?"

"Because by then I resented you."

"I'd have moved the earth for you. I hope you know that."

He lowered his eyes.

"I don't forgive you. At all. I can't. You hurt me, Theo, and you didn't even have the face to do it yourself."

"Costumes please, actors. Costumes."

We both turned towards the call.

"I'm sorry, Cassidy," he said.

I couldn't look at him anymore. I wanted this conversation to end, so I held my hand out to him. He sighed as he shook my hand.

"Just..." I shrugged. "Just allow yourself to be *you*. If that means being under the radar, doing theatre, then that's what that means. Don't take someone else down to succeed. It isn't worth it."

I wasn't on until about halfway through the first act, but it went so quickly; the hours and hours of rehearsal were almost unfathomable. The time we'd spent to perfect a minute on stage. How quickly the show was over even though it had just begun.

I stood in the wings watching the show until I was required on stage. Finn was in the opposite wing, his book in his hand, a little light shining on the script, a pair of comms on because he wasn't going to let this show run without his input.

He noticed me during the song before I was due on. He pulled his tongue at me, so I laughed quietly, pulling a face back before crossing both of my fingers. He nodded, blowing a kiss to me and touching his chest. I took a deep breath, waited for the blackout and stepped onto the stage.

The lights came up sharply, and I was stood tall above Theo on the floor. How the audience reacted; they screamed and hooted at me, the noise travelling, and I let myself smile as my eyes scanned the top of the theatre, then right back down to the orchestra pit. I saw Cody first, his cello poised, ready to play, then I looked across to Kennedy as he stood facing me, although he wasn't supposed to be. His saxophone was raised and he had a smile on his face.

He caught my eye and waved at me. I nodded back an ever so slight movement, and then I began to sing.

Finn accompanied me to the Golden Boys show. I had told him I was going alone, and he wasn't happy at all with that so he offered to come along with me. After of course we'd finished crying over the last night of my last show.

Finn had been in awe when we walked into the Goldstein Hall. He hadn't stopped telling me about *this* show he'd done, and *that* show he'd done. Little memories and anecdotes about his time as a Golden Boy.

Max, Cameron's boyfriend, had found me and sat next to me with a few of his ballet friends. They were all as immersed in Finn's stories as I was. He only stopped when the doors at the back of the hall opened and the orchestra walked through the audience, line by line.

Nick was in the first line, as he went straight to the back of the orchestra pit to sit at his drums, the other boy in his line sitting himself at the piano.

The next line appeared to be mostly strings. Cellos and violins and violas. Then, the brass section came in.

I had tried to persuade Kennedy to come with me. I had used the allure of the orchestra in my attempt. He'd declined, telling me that Stephen had his last match of the season tonight and he kind of had to be there as his boyfriend.

I had accepted that. Kind of.

Casper took his seat with his trumpet, looking through the sheet music before him and not looking at the audience at all.

243

Their show was an original masterpiece, written and produced by their seventh year class. Finn had told me it was supposed to show their personalities, it was meant to be a showcase of their talents, of who they were and what their journey in the school had been like.

I couldn't take my eyes off the stage as Harley and Thomas took on the lead roles.

I stood with the rest of the audience at the finale, cheering and clapping loudly with Finn and Max as the entire cast shared a hug on stage, all of them laughing with tears running down their cheeks. Much like I had been at my curtain call last night whilst Archie had cuddled firmly into my side as I said goodbye.

My cheers got somehow louder when the orchestra ran up the steps to join them on the stage, all of them sharing hugs before standing in a line, their arms wrapped around each other's waists as they sang the last chorus of their finale song.

I met Casper at the stage door, as he didn't have to get changed after the curtain call. He came to me, still in his uniform, his hair gelled back, his shirt tucked in.

I wrapped my arms around him, hugging him tightly before pulling on the bottom of his shirt. He laughed, wiggling away from me, then messed up his hair. It was sticking up because of the gel.

"Couldn't persuade your brother?" he asked as he looked towards Max, then Finn, his expression almost confused.

"He had to fulfil boyfriend duties. It's okay. We'll

figure it out but once I told Finn I was coming to a Golden Boy show, there was no going back," I said in a laugh as Finn waved.

"Finn," Casper repeated then smirked, "your theatre teacher."

"My *ex*-theatre teacher," I said. "Now, I believe he's just my friend." I looked back at Finn as he nodded.

"Exactly that. You were amazing by the way. Not as good as my boys this week, but amazing."

"Of course," Casper said, laughing as Finn nodded to us both, then excused himself to go and talk to their teachers.

Harley and Cameron appeared next, both still glowing with their stage makeup, but in t-shirts with their school logo on the chest and joggers.

We began applauding them the moment we saw them, Cameron laughing shyly before disappearing into Max's waiting arms.

Harley came to me.

"You were…" I shook my head. "Incredible," I told him, then curtseyed.

"You're the Queen, you don't curtsey for anyone," he said in a gasp.

I touched my chest. "I curtsey for other Queens," I informed him, grinning at him as he blushed then held his hands out to me, so I hugged him, barely letting go of him when we cheered for Thomas, as he came through the door with Nick.

I left their post-show party at midnight as I knew if I

didn't leave then, I wouldn't have left until the next morning and I wanted to spend my last night in my dorm room.

Kennedy had had the same idea as he was sat up on his phone waiting for me to come back.

"I'd have thought you'd have stayed with Stephen," I said as I began to dress for bed. Cody laughed from his bed, shaking his head at me as Kennedy did.

"On our last night? Definitely not," he replied as he stood from his bed. "This'll probably be the last night I ever share a room with you again, never mind it actually being the last night in this school. I'm spending it with you."

I hugged him. I squeezed him tightly, burying my face into his shoulder, then laughed when Cody's arms came around us.

"I didn't want to be left out," he whispered directly into my ear, so I squeezed him tight, too. Kennedy broke the hug when he realised I was crying. He wiped his thumbs over my cheeks, smiling at me as he shook his head.

"It's going to be okay."

"I know," I told him, nodding as I swallowed down the tears. "I know. These are complicated tears. Like, goodbye tears. They're not necessarily sad."

"How was the show?" he whispered.

I nodded, wiping my own cheeks quickly. "It was *amazing*," I answered. "Incredible. I'm going to have some competition in my new house," I said. He laughed happily before scooping me back up in another cuddle.

"Did Stephen win?"

"Of course," he whispered straight into my ear, "of course he did. Got man of the match, too. He's already told me that he expects a game against Casper though. Apparently the seven years of Casper's team beating their asses isn't forgotten about easily."

I laughed.

"I'm sure we can arrange that," I told him.

There really weren't as many boxes as we had expected, but I supposed that's what happened when you moved out of a boarding school.

We'd moved our clothes in and any small things we'd accumulated over the years, then we'd sat on the floor of our living room with a pizza to celebrate moving in, as we had very little else to do.

The house already had most of the base furniture and, besides making our beds – which we were all putting off doing – there was nothing to do but eat pizza.

"I've spoken to my mum," Harley said as he scrolled through his phone with one hand, whilst trying not to drop any of his pizza onto his baby pink dungarees with the other. "She said she's going to hold my stuff hostage until I come visit," he smirked, "so I think I'm going home with her after graduation."

"Home alone," I teased to Casper. He winked at me.

"Apparently my stuff will arrive this week in a moving truck. Dad's sent all my stuff here. They're sending Cam's when they get back from Portugal." He shrugged. "I guess we'll just have to live in simplicity for

247

a little while. That okay, Queen?" he asked, grinning at me.

I rose my piece of pizza. "I think I'll be just fine," I told Casper, then looked at Harley as he examined me. "I saw your speakers come with you. As long as we have the *Waitress* soundtrack at least once a day, I'll be fine."

Harley laughed, clapping as he agreed with me.

"I think me and you are going to have a very beautiful friendship, Cassidy Bradford," he said. I winked at him.

We finally got around to putting our bedsheets on when we were on our way to bed. We both sighed when we walked into the bare bed with the folded sheets resting on top of them. I glanced at Casper. He looked back at me.

His eyes darkened almost instantly and I couldn't have him looking like *that* in my direction, so I grabbed him, pulling him towards me and kissing him deeply, feeling as a laugh rumbled in his throat before I pushed him back onto the bare bed.

"You get the sheet, I'll do the pillows?" he said, lifting the bedsheets to me. I took them from him, throwing them onto the floor next to the bed before kneeling above him. He pulled his tongue up to me. I caught it in a kiss almost instantly.

We'd slept together a month ago, after dancing around each other for a little longer than necessary. A blowjob here, a handjob there, a little bit of innocent dry humping, but never letting it go any further.

Not until a Saturday date we had three weeks or so after he'd shown me the house for the first time.

We were in his dorm, having decided not to go out and do anything. He of course had his trumpet gig later that night but until then we lay in his bed, watching a Netflix series on his laptop.

We'd definitely stopped concentrating on it, but could you blame me as he lay next to me, his t-shirt riding up, so the band of his boxers was exposed along with some skin, his fingers stroking over my thighs and knees almost absently.

Soon we were kissing, and hands were in pants.

Then clothes were on the floor and one thing had led to another.

When we'd arrived for his gig that night, he was giddy. Everyone had known *instantly* that we'd slept together that afternoon.

His fingers stroked down my stomach before he pushed himself up by his elbows. I leant down so my face was closer to his, his eyes tracking mine before he whispered, "I want you to fuck me tonight."

I smiled at him, moving closer so we could kiss again, my hands lifting the bottom of his t-shirt as his worked on my pants. He growled, frustrated at me as he struggled with my button, knocking his head against my cheek as he looked down between us, trying to open my jeans.

I laughed above him, my hands in his hair as I knelt a little higher, giving him more room to work with. A triumphant cheer came out of him when he managed to pull my jeans off. He pushed them down as best he could before I kicked them off.

"Well done," I teased. He gasped up at me, so I pulled my tongue back at him, moving my head away from him as he tried to catch my tongue. "Hey," I whispered, moving closer to him again. He nodded as my fingers threaded through his hair. "You sure you want me on top?"

"I'm sure," he whispered back to me. I smirked as I grabbed for his hair. He gasped, the sound surprised, so I winked at him, tilting his head away from me and kissing his neck, enjoying his sighs above as I got lower, kissing his Adam's apple then back up to his ear.

"Don't leave a hickey," he whispered. I laughed against his neck, feeling him shiver when my breath touched him. "I can't have a hickey on graduation."

"Of course not," I murmured straight into his ear. "I would never..." I licked his earlobe. He moaned lightly. "Give you a visible hickey before graduation," I added, then began down his chest, until I reached his stomach. I looked up at him, smirking as he watched me with blown eyes.

His entire body raised from the bed when I began to suck on his stomach.

I licked around the hickey when I lifted my head away, glancing up at him as he took long deep breaths in. He raised his hand and showed me the condom he'd obviously fished out of somewhere when my mouth was occupied.

It had been like relearning how to have sex with him, because everything had felt so different; everything felt so

I *knew* how to have sex. I'd been having sex for years, but a lot of my sex had been faced down on a mattress, face stuffed into a pillow. Or up against a desk, or a wall. A quick fumble that led to an easy orgasm, with no other intention.

The first time I'd slept with Casper, we were slow. We moved delicately and carefully; we talked through everything we did. We held each other close, we looked into each other's eyes with every movement. We kissed as we came.

Sure, it had been quick and hot once or twice. We'd been left alone for an amount of time and suddenly clothes were flying and we were fumbling over a condom with slick hands trying to get the *damn* thing to open.

But every time had given me something different, every time I learnt something new about myself, about how I liked to have sex. About Casper's body, his kinks, his sweet spots. About how he whimpered if I kissed his neck. How he shuddered something rotten if I panted into his ear as we came.

"Cassidy," he whispered into my ear, my hair wrapped tightly around his fingers, his forehead against mine as he tried to keep his eyes open, his mouth open but no sound coming out.

He was beautiful and I told him as much, feeling him shiver against me, his small gasps of delight at the compliments.

He repeated my name, over and over until he came, gasping deeply, then kissing me as deeply. He held my

251

face in his hands as he tried to keep a rhythm going, his movements sporadic and clumsy, so I lay him back into the bed. I only needed to move into him a few more times before I came myself.

His fingers ran through my hair, a laugh playing on his expression before pulling me close again and kissing me, with just lips.

I fell onto the bed beside him, kissing his shoulder before nestling my head into it.

"I love you," I whispered into his shoulder, kissing it again then biting my lip as I closed my eyes.

Because I'd said it first.

He rose his shoulder, lifting my chin with it, then turned so he was lying facing me.

"Say that again," he said in a gasp. I shook my head quickly as he laughed softly. "Cassidy," he whispered. I looked at him. "Say it again."

"I love you," I whispered back. He practically beamed, moving closer to me, leaning his forehead against mine, his fingers stroking over my chest before he rose his eyes so he was looking straight at me.

"I love you," he told me. I exhaled, seeing his smile, a delicate thing that was *definitely* meant just for me.

"Say it again," I whispered back.

Nineteen

Our graduation was a cap-and-gown kind of affair. Although uncommon for leaving a secondary school, Ravenwood thought it necessary to celebrate their leavers. That and if you didn't pass your final exams you *didn't* get to wear the fancy cap and gown.

Kennedy and I had passed. I'd guessed, since a cap and gown had been delivered to both of us – but I would also suppose that there'd be an uproar if the King and Queen didn't graduate.

They'd been delivered to our parents' house.

I'd received a text from my mum telling me and asking whether I wanted to come and collect it, or if she should bring it to my house.

I'd asked Kennedy what he was doing and he informed me he'd received a phone call from Father *telling* him he was to pick up his gown.

I told Mum I would pick it up on my own, as I felt it was only fair to Kennedy.

I had toyed with inviting Casper along with me, but decided I didn't want to put him into that kind of situation.

I needn't have worried.

"He's not coming," Kennedy said as he sat on the kitchen counter next to Mum who was making cinnamon buns, a childhood favourite of Kennedy's and mine. We'd have buns bigger than our heads, drizzled with icing and orange curls. Our faces would end up sticky, our fingers more so.

Mum made them whenever we visited for Christmas. *I* assume she'd make them whenever we visit full stop from now on.

"It's the election tomorrow," Mum said. She sounded as if she and Father had exchanged words about this numerous times. "He has to be visible, show his face to get the votes." She sighed then turned to me. "Your scandal costed him a few points on the poll."

"For real?" Kennedy asked as I laughed.

"*Scandal*," I repeated. Kennedy smirked at me. "Casper will relish in that."

"He came across badly," she said then, "but I'm so *glad* you refused to go on that date. Mostly for yourself, and your relationship – I want to meet him by the way – but I feel your father would've come off worse if you'd been photographed on a date. It'd have felt forced and would've really ruined his chances, especially after everyone seeing you with Casper in the magazine."

"So, no he isn't coming," Kennedy repeated.

She shook her head. "No, he's not attending your

graduation. Harrison is though."

"Good," I said quietly then looked up. "Good that Harrison is coming."

"Do you think he's going to win?" Kennedy asked.

Mum sighed. "I wouldn't want to comment on the matter," she answered. "Things will change if he does, you both know that."

"I'm not changing my mind," I said.

She turned to me, shaking her head. "No, I can't imagine you will. I fully respect your decision; I just don't want you to lose touch."

"With you, never," I said, and she smiled before looking at Kennedy.

"Your life will be a bit more complicated."

"Stephen has no contact with his mother, so either nothing will change, or Father will be prime minister," he said softly then looked between us. "Either way, we'll be in Amsterdam until further notice."

"And then what?" I asked.

He sighed. "I don't know. Well, *I* do. Stephen's starting with the fire service."

"Excuse me, Stephen is not allowed to be that hot without prior knowledge."

"Stephen has *always* been that hot," Kennedy informed me. I laughed as he smirked.

"And what are you going to do?" Mum asked, waving her hand at the both of us as she obviously didn't want to weigh in on the hotness of Stephen.

"Audition for some orchestras, I guess."

"I know a place you can gig," I told him, hitting his

knees with enthusiasm. "And it gives me a chance to finally properly introduce you to Casper."

I took a deep breath as I tied my bowtie whilst watching my reflection. My room was practically ready to be put in the back of a van. Everything in a box except my bed and my mirror.

Even though I hadn't slept in my bed last night, I'd slept in Kennedy's, whispering with him into the dead of night before finally falling asleep because his room wasn't in boxes. He wasn't taking most of his childhood bedroom with him – he intended to come back and stay sometimes.

I didn't.

I finished tying my bowtie, straightened my braces, then closed my eyes.

"You ready?" Kennedy whispered from behind me, his arms wrapping around me protectively. I kissed his thumb.

"I'm ready," I muttered. "Let me see what you're wearing."

"It's graduation," he stated as I turned and lifted his arms, gasping at the far too simple white shirt and black tie. "We can't all pull off baby pink and, what are we calling the colour of your pants, beige?"

"How dare you."

He bit his lip, obviously trying to stop himself from laughing. He turned when my door opened with a knock.

"The car's here," Harrison said as he examined the both of us. He almost looked proud.

"I'm surprised you're not at Mister Prime Minister's side today," I said as I picked up my phone. I glanced at it as it lit up, smiling at the top message from Casper.

"This is far more important," he said. I looked up towards him. "Far, far more important. Now come on, the car's here."

We all left my room, finding Mum at the bottom of the stairs.

"Don't you both just look so grown up," she said in a sigh as she looked us both over. "Now come on," she added quickly, directing us out of the door towards the town car.

We were robed and photographed almost the moment we set foot in the grounds. Harrison and our mum were taken to their seats while we were told to hold diplomas and smile. We did, together, apart, together again then we were led to our class.

Kennedy had to make a speech. Granted, I'd written it for him, but he had to stand before everyone and make a speech as the King. He closed the entire ceremony. He turned around to hug Otis, his orchestra teacher, as we all stood and cheered for him.

"This is nothing like *High School Musical Three*," Cody said to me as he also clapped for Kennedy. "Where is the musical number?" he added. I laughed.

"I can arrange that for you," I told him; he knocked our elbows against each other's before wrapping me up in a hug.

"So, King Malakai, can I tell everyone yet?" Archie

asked, so I turned, gasping, and picked him up in a hug. He laughed into my ear, squeezing me back. When I put him back on the floor he was crying. "I'm going to miss you so much."

"You've got this," I said as I wiped his tears. "Honestly. You'll rule someday, Archie."

"Yeah, King Arthur, I'm sure I've heard that somewhere before," he teased.

"With your King Consort," I teased right back. He blushed.

"With my King Consort."

"You can call or text me whenever, I promise I'll pick up. Even if you just want to talk, or tell me the latest gossip. Anything, Archie, okay?"

"Okay," he said, the tears rolling down his cheeks again.

"And I'm sure Kennedy will allow you to break the news of the new King," I said as Kennedy walked towards us. Archie looked up at him almost starry eyed.

"Kennedy will allow what?" he repeated, frowning at me as I grinned at Archie.

"The new King announcement of course. Archie is itching to tell everyone," I said as I wrapped my arms around his shoulders, swinging Archie side to side. He laughed, burying his head into my arm.

"You can definitely spread the news. Only right that a future King tell everyone the news."

Archie buried his head into me further, shaking his head as he laughed.

"Shouldn't you be in class, Archie?"

We turned together as Finn stood smirking at us. Archie sighed dramatically.

"I had to see my Queen, of course."

"Of course," Finn agreed. "Now go to Maths."

"Wow, he's becoming tough now you're leaving," Archie said then hugged me properly, kissing my cheek and grinning at me before walking back towards the school. Finn winked at me, making me laugh as I turned to search through the crowd. I stopped when I landed on Devon.

I went to him. He jumped when I touched his shoulder.

"Hey," I said quietly. He glanced at me before looking away.

"Hey. Guess I graduated. That wasn't expected, huh?" he said. I smiled at him; his smile back was a fragile thing.

"How are you feeling?" I asked.

He sighed but nodded. "I'm okay. Honestly. I feel really okay and just that, but…"

"That's okay," we said together. He nodded.

"Spending summer with my parents before moving down to uni." His nod slowed. "Thank you, you know, for that night."

"You're very welcome."

The café that Casper performed in was holding a student night event to encourage students to vote in the election and then watch it. Hunter was on the door, making us promise we'd cast our vote before even letting us through the door.

When we stepped in all the small televisions were on, showing us projections and exit polls but all of them muted because he wanted to encourage performances – and that was why we were here, Kennedy with his saxophone in tow and Stephen because I couldn't not invite him.

Casper was already in the café when I was finally allowed entry, sat beside Cameron, his trumpet on the seat between them.

"This is about to get really weird, isn't it?" Stephen said as he examined them. I laughed, reaching my hands out in front of me. As expected, Casper grabbed for them, letting me stand him up and kiss him.

"How was graduation?" he asked.

"It was like a graduation," I said in a laugh. "I'm free now, though, free of school, free of home, free of everything." I squeezed his hand in mine. "I can move everything in tomorrow whilst you're wearing the pretty cap and gown."

He nodded to me, squeezing my hand back, then looked behind me so I turned.

"Kennedy," I said before turning to Casper. "I believe you two know each other."

"Yes," Kennedy said as he put his saxophone case on the table, "you're in competition with both me and my boyfriend."

Casper's eyes jumped from Kennedy to Stephen. He laughed.

"Oh, the Ravens goalie," he said, his voice taking on

a mocking tone.

Stephen smirked back at him. "The Hawks striker..." He tilted his head. "I've saved every one of your goals, I believe."

"Shut up," Casper muttered; Stephen laughed.

"Still beat you for seven years, didn't we," Zack said. We turned together as Stephen nodded, examining Zack, Nick, and Thomas with his eyes.

"True, true, but we took home the championship this year didn't we?"

Zack scoffed, pushing Stephen's shoulder as he laughed back at them. I exchanged a look with Kennedy.

"I think that means they're getting along," Cameron said, so I looked at him. "I think that's what it says in my football talk handbook."

"You need to get me a copy of that," I told him.

"Let's get tonight started," Hunter said into the microphone. "Bradford is currently ahead in the Exit Poll."

I moaned as Kennedy sighed.

"So let's have some music." He held his hands out to us as if telling us we could choose who goes first.

"Go on Raven," Casper said. Kennedy cocked an eyebrow at him. "Show us what you're made of."

Kennedy scoffed, reaching past us to get his saxophone from the table and stepping up onto the stage. Hunter eyed him curiously.

"You're new," he said, then turned towards me. "Right?"

"Right," we agreed. Hunter nodded, holding his

hands up, and stepped off the stage as Kennedy prepared his saxophone. He winked at me then began to play.

"Wow," Cameron whispered as Thomas sat beside him, nodding up to Kennedy.

"Wow," he agreed.

Casper shrugged beside me. "He's okay."

I pushed his shoulder. He laughed, grabbing hold of my hand, and pulled me towards him.

"How do you feel?" he whispered to me, looking up towards the TV as the blue graph grew.

"Nervous," I said with a nod. "But, it's okay." I took a breath. "It'll be fine."

"I'll make sure of it," he said, kissing my cheek.

"Who are we backing here?" Nick asked, looking up towards the TV himself. "I voted for neither of them, but who do we want to win? Are we team Cassidy's Dad?"

"I'm not," I said.

He glanced at me. "Really?"

I laughed in a shrug. "I don't want him to win."

"Even though he's your dad, you want Amelia to beat him?"

"Yeah," I confirmed.

"I, on the other hand, want the complete opposite," Stephen said. "I'd love Cassidy's dad to beat my mum."

Nick looked between us. "Is this normal?"

"Happens after years of rejection," Stephen said with a shrug. "If she loses, she might start spending time with me again. Who knows?" he said, then began to applaud Kennedy as he laughed on the stage.

"You don't like your parents?" Nick asked.

Stephen shrugged. "No."

"I like my mum," I told him; he shook his head, slowly turning to Thomas.

"I can't even imagine."

"Count yourself lucky then," Thomas said softly before kissing Nick's cheek.

"Come on drummer boy," Casper said in a laugh, taking Nick's hand. "Let's give the saxophone some company." He tugged on Nick who went willingly, pulling his drumsticks out of his pocket as he jumped up onto the stage.

Kennedy laughed happily, watching them with interest before huddling close to Casper, whispering between the two of them. Casper took a few steps back, winked at Kennedy then began to play.

I stepped next to Stephen.

"I think they get along," Stephen said with a nod. "I know you were worried about that."

"He didn't know."

"No," Stephen said with a laugh. "He didn't realise that he was worrying you every time he rescheduled meeting Casper, but he also wasn't doing it on purpose."

"I *know* the King has his duties. I was well aware."

"But you wanted your brother to meet your boyfriend," he said with a smirk. "He was as nervous for you to find out about me. Remember?"

"I do," I said quietly. "I do. It wasn't that I didn't think he'd *like* him. I guess I just didn't think they were each other's kind of person."

"And you think *I'm* your kind of person?"

263

"True," I said in a laugh. He grinned. He knocked his arm against mine.

"Did you figure out your word?"

"I did," I muttered, then nodded. "I am definitely genderqueer and I kind of love it."

"I'm so happy for you," he said then cleared his throat.

"Thank you, sweetheart," I whispered, kissing his cheek.

"Good luck tonight," he murmured, nodding towards the TV. The blue side of the graph continued to grow; a lot of the country map was also coloured in blue. I took a breath.

"You, too," I said. "I hope the result gives you what you want from your mother."

"I'll never get what I want from my mother." He looked at me. "I gave up hoping for that when she took on a second term."

"When you were fourteen?"

"Exactly. I'll be fine whatever the result." He squeezed my hand. "I hope you will, too."

I looked around the bar as Thomas and Zack cheered upon Harley's arrival at the café, beckoning him in and to their table. Cameron laughed with them as he looked from his phone, probably at a text from Max towards them.

Then I turned to the stage as Casper clapped Kennedy as he bowed, then stood and clapped right back at Casper as he also bowed.

"You know what…" Stephen glanced at me as they

both turned to applaud Nick. "I think I'll be *just* fine," I said, then turned as I was beckoned onto the stage.

"The stage awaits you, Queen," Stephen said.

I turned to him just before I stepped onto the stage. "I'm not the Queen anymore." I turned as Casper held his hand out to help me up. I took the microphone. "I'm just Cassidy."

AUTHORS NOTE

Hi! I've never written an author's note before, or should I say, I've never felt the need to but Cassidy, well Cassidy Bradford is different. I, however, can't talk about Cassidy without talking about Kennedy first, because he is where this all began.

I wrote Kennedy is King *back in 2019; the building blocks simply being 'what if I turned the popularity trope on its head'. That was all, no storyline, no characters, nothing. Just that simple idea which, of course, evolved and became what we now know as the Ravenwood books. But Ravenwood didn't start there, no Ravenwood started way back in 2017, with Harrison and Preston and a story of grief, loss, and depression because 2017 was a particularly low time for me and I dealt with it the only way I could, through writing.*

Their story was a particularly dark one, and one that was never meant to be read, not by anyone. By the time I was writing Kennedy, the dark spell was on its way out and I will forever be grateful I came out the other side, but I knew Preston and Harrison's story was an extremely important one, so I kept it in my back pocket waiting for the right time.

Preston featured in Teen Heaven, *my debut as Cameron*

James back in early 2020 (I know yikes!), and along with him we saw Ravenwood again, but I knew that wasn't anywhere near enough. Fast forward (or I suppose back!) to writing Kennedy, and the plot line was starting to come together — shout out to my springboard Jess, who built this story from the ground up with me — we'd decided on Stephen, the trans footballer love interest, and Otis, the ex-King orchestra teacher, and of course Kennedy and Cassidy, the twins that rule the school as King and Queen, but something was missing. To us it was 'what is the event that pulls these two together?' What is the 'there's only one bed' or the 'forced proximity' that traps our King and his footballer into forced conversation, forced time together. A bike ride! But why are they doing a bike ride? What is the reason.

The conversation went something like; they could be raising money. What for though? The school. Eh... oh, what if they're raising money for Preston. Yes like a whole school thing. Yes, yes but what if it's deeper than that. How? Maybe Preston was their brother? No, that's not right... Harrison. Harrison!

Sometimes in writing things just make sense; Harrison being Kennedy and Cassidy's older brother, and Preston's story being intwined with theirs made everything fall into place. This brought about the discussions around modern-day HIV, including PrEP and relationships — which I think is an extremely important topic that should feature in contemporary stories, and the discussion around mental health, and suicide, both tough subjects that are prominent in young people's lives. Sure, neither of these things are pivotal to the plot — bike ride aside — but they are *underlaying through the story, as they are with life.*

So, we're off to a flying start, typing away, the story practically writing itself, but in the back of my mind there was Cassidy. Cassidy, so much Cassidy. There was more to the story about Cassidy. I practically wrote the conclusion of Kennedy and opened up a new document and started Cassidy is Queen.

With Cassidy, I knew exactly the story I wanted, that I needed to tell and I was finally ready to tell it. Cassidy was always going to be a bit more risqué; Cassidy definitely had more tricks up his sleeve and had heaps more experience. Cassidy's story was never going to be an A – B love story, no way. I knew I wanted to explore Cassidy's gender, because Cassidy had never felt cisgender to me, and I wanted to make sure I gave him my full attention. I wanted to make sure we, together, found his word.

Because gender, woo-ee that was a big one, but the sparks notes, I've never felt much like my gender assigned at birth. I'd known this since I was 13, but I didn't address it until 10 years later when I came out as trans (not quite!), and then a year after that when I came out as nonbinary (Ding! Ding! Ding!) It was a different feeling altogether; learning my word, feeling comfortable in it, and knowing it was the right one.

It was that feeling I wanted to recreate through Cassidy, and his journey to find the word he didn't even know he was looking for, because that's important too. I saw on Twitter once, someone saying 'you don't have to be miserable to transition', and it's true, sometimes we get so hung up on the small arguments like, do you need dysphoria to be trans? Should you have always known? That we forget sometimes that everyone's experience with gender, and transitioning is different and unique to that person.

This was what I wanted Cassidy to experience; finding a word that fit him but not even knowing he was looking, for him to find another person who had already been on that journey, and who could be a comfort, a hand to hold whilst he explored terminology and tried things on for size. Someone who wasn't there to judge, or to pressure him into a label, and that person could only ever be Casper.

Have I mentioned how this book is full to the brim of cameos of characters I once wrote — almost like the long-lost friends parade at the Magic Kingdom. The Golden Boys had their time in the sun many years ago with Casper and Cameron (name check!) at the helm. You may also recognise Max as the father of my ballet dancer Jacob from Light as a Feather.

But I digress. The coupling of Cassidy and Casper together was a lightbulb moment I couldn't believe I hadn't thought of before. I mean it was right there, and how else were they supposed to meet besides a coffee shop mix-up, and yes, it blossomed into romance and yes, they became partners, but their relationship was so much more because for the first time in Cassidy's life, he had found someone who was real with him, who liked him for who he was and didn't entertain his Queen persona.

Ah yes, popularity strikes again, because gender was just one part of Cassidy's story, the other of course being his Queendom, and how his friends were simply followers, how no-one wanted Cassidy, but needed *the Queen. How none of his relationships before Casper really had meaning, or any weight to them. How the power is all consuming, and easy to fall victim to (see: relationship with Finn). How, when the time comes, that friends are needed, they're not there.*

Which brings me onto Devon. Devon who I knew from the beginning was never going to be as black and white as a bitch with a complex, but who I was working on in the background because I fully believe there's always more to a person than just their vindictive actions, and with that we full circle back to the inclusion of Preston in these stories; the importance of Preston's story, and the impact his suicide had on not only the school, but on the Bradford family. The memories Cassidy holds from that time, and the empathy he carries even as everything around him falls apart. The bigger picture that Cassidy sees that allows him to forgive, and comfort the once villain in his, and his brothers story. How Cassidy was the bigger person, and helped Devon at his darkest moment, when he simply could've left him alone.

Cassidy was always a very complex character to me, and I felt that didn't come through fully in Kennedy is King. *He definitely has more layers than his brother, and a lot more complicated feelings, and thoughts regarding their popularity, his self-worth, romance, and his riches.*

I put a lot of myself into Cassidy, allowing him as a character to explore, and discuss things that I'd experienced, and were important to me. I have a huge soft-spot for my Queen — he is one of a handful of my characters that I can see myself in and would open a fresh document to write over and over.

Believe me, whenever I'm writing a new story the question of 'can I wiggle a Cassidy cameo in here?' comes up far more than you'd think!

I could talk forever about Cassidy, and I am definitely willing to. The subject of Cassidy is definitely a 'once I've started, I can't stop' kind of one, but for now, their Ravenwood chapter is closed. Kennedy and Cassidy's that is, there are plenty more Ravenwood stories but that's in the hands of their heirs.

So for a piece of mind; Kennedy and Stephen do get married, when they're 25. Kennedy has a regular gig as a saxophonist at a local club, and Stephen has passed his test to become a firefighter. Kennedy grows the beard he's always wanted, and they adopted a little girl together. Kennedy does still talk to his parents but isn't supported financially by them.

Cassidy goes straight into auditioning for off-West End, and West End productions, whilst Casper secures a spot in a West End orchestra. Soon, Cassidy is hired as an ensemble member before taking on a lead role (I see him as May in &Juliet!). When Cassidy and Casper are in their late 20s, they decide to make the move to New York taking Broadway by storm, and living out their lives together over there, in a very happily-ever-after kind of way. Cassidy never speaks to his father again, but he does send regular updates to his mum.

Now, for the non-fictional stuff. I want to say a huge thank you to Jess for putting up with my fictional worlds for 11+ years now! I also want to shout out Drew, your support means the world to me, honestly, and last, but by no means least, I want to say a huge thank you to Lottie for being the most supportive and loving partner and being the ultimate fangirl 😊 who will always be as, if not more, excited than me to see my books on the shelves – I mean, Kennedy is kind of the reason we got together, but that's a story for another day.

Lastly, I want to say thank you to all of you, the readers who bought Cassidy and supported me on this journey, I literally couldn't do this without you.

I hope you all find your words, and live your happily ever afters.

SRL Publishing don't just publish books, we also do our best in keeping this world sustainable. In the UK alone, over 77 million books are destroyed each year, unsold and unread, due to overproduction and bigger profit margins.

Our business model is inherently sustainable by only printing what we sell. While this means our cost price is much higher, it means we have minimum waste and zero returns. We made a public promise in 2020 to never overprint our books just for the sake of profit.

We give back to our planet by calculating the number of trees used for our products so we can then replace. We also calculate our carbon emissions and support projects which reduce CO_2. These same projects also support the United Nations Sustainable Development Goals.

The way we operate means we knowingly waive our profit margins for the sake of the environment. Every book sold via the SRL website plants at least one tree.

To find out more, please visit
www.srlpublishing.co.uk/responsibility